THE MAN
IN THE
RIVER

BY JAMES DUFFY

Missing
The Revolt of the Teddy Bears
The Christmas Gang
Cleaver of the Good Luck Diner

THE MAN IN THE RIVER

JAMES DUFFY

CHARLES SCRIBNER'S SONS
NEW YORK

Charles Scribner's Sons Books for Young Readers
Macmillan Publishing Company
866 Third Avenue, New York, NY 10022
Collier Macmillan Canada, Inc.

Printed in the United States of America
First Edition   10 9 8 7 6 5 4 3 2 1

Library of Congress Cataloging-in-Publication Data
Duffy, James, date.
The man in the river / James Duffy. — 1st ed.   p.   cm.
Summary: Twelve-year-old Sandy and ten-year-old Kate, whose father has become the town drunk, receive investigative help from a retired policewoman when their father drowns mysteriously in the river after beginning to make a new life for himself.
[1. Mystery and detective stories.]   I. Title.
PZ7.D87814Man 1990   [Fic]—dc20   89–10200 CIP AC
ISBN 0–684–19161–X

For Robert Manners

THE MAN IN THE RIVER

1

The raspberry canes were a tangled mess. Was it worth it? Agatha Bates asked herself. Was she really so fond of raspberries that she should try to disentangle the thorny brush and cut it back to the ground, the way Arthur Harper had told her to do?

"You can't kill them," he had said to Agatha when they met in front of the general store. "They're hard to dig up, and they won't die and go away, either. You're stuck with them, so you might as well tame them. Be sure to wear leather gloves. They have awful thorns. You get them healthy again, Agatha, and I'll help you pick them." He laughed. "Alice can make me some jelly."

Agatha had told him that if she got the plants producing, she'd pick the berries herself and make her own jelly. She had gone back into the store and asked Mr. Reed for the toughest work gloves he had and a pair of sturdy clippers. Things like gloves and clippers were a lot cheaper in the mall, but it was over twenty miles away, and, like almost everyone else in Wingate, New Hampshire, Agatha felt a

1

responsibility to keep the general store going so it would always be there when she needed it.

She knelt down now to start cutting the canes. The soil was still frozen an inch under the surface, a pale ground-frost holding the hard clumps of earth together. Agatha grumbled to herself that spring never really came to Wingate. Spring was mud and dead leaves and a chimney that wouldn't draw the smoke from the fireplace into the soggy, chill air outside. She reminded herself again to rake the leaves away from the daffodils along the walk when she finished with the raspberries. Yesterday she had noticed the first green spikes forcing themselves up through the packed maple leaves.

She supposed Henry had done all these things when he came to the cottage alone those weekends when she was on duty. She couldn't remember ever working in the garden or around the edges of the cottage to clear away winter's trash and trim the roses back to their thick, green stems. What her memory told her was of the summer season, the years when the children were still with them and the golden years afterward. She saw the garden growing, the roses blooming, and the grass, trimmed and verdant, stretching from the street to the door. In her mind's eye, she and Henry sat on the side porch and took their lunch or tea, rejoicing gently, it seemed to her now, in the miracle of their life together. They watched the yellow tomcat stalk the school playing field for a mouse or mole, always with an eye out for Arthur's golden retriever, who chased cats as well as rabbits and squirrels. Henry and the retriever were gone. Agatha remained behind, along with Tom, curled up next to the radiator in the living room.

She should have learned a little about gardening then, Agatha supposed, but there was never enough time just to be with Henry and the children. Their days together had slipped away or been stolen away by the calls from the Boston police department to tell her she was needed to help out with this or that emergency in the precinct.

Well, no calls were coming in now, when she needed them. She was aware that some thorns had already worked their way through the leather into her fingers. It was time to stop.

Agatha felt pretty good as she opened a can of chicken soup. The exercise had made her aware of her body again. Her back was stiff, but that would go away. After lunch, she'd take her nap and then rake the leaves off the daffodils. And tomorrow? She'd see about tomorrow when it came.

She picked up the Boston paper. There at the top of the page, staring at her, was the ugly face of Detective Lieutenant Andy Flynn, known as Handy Andy in the precinct. He had been indicted, Agatha read, for accepting money from merchants for unspecified services that they never received. Poor Andy. Agatha shook her head. He was the ugly sweetheart of the station. Every day he delivered coffee and doughnuts. More than that, when he was Agatha's partner he had once saved her life.

He had pushed her out of the way of a hoodlum's car when it came roaring out of the alley where they had pursued him. The hoodlum ran his car into Andy and the wall before Andy could skip clear. He had a small limp forever after from a broken knee. Following the accident, Andy seemed to get fat. He must have figured the merchants owed him something for his bum knee.

Was there someone at the door? Agatha Bates put the paper down and listened. There was someone. She heard the slight tap of someone who was embarrassed to knock any louder. Any noise at the door was a surprise. Agatha couldn't remember when there had been a knock at the door during the dreary winter months. Arthur and Alice Harper from next door just walked in. Malcolm Torbert, the police chief, had come by a month or so ago to see if everything was all right. He hadn't knocked; he had shouted. And that was everyone who visited. Agatha hurried to the door.

Lydia Prescott was standing on the stoop in plastic boots, an old raincoat, and a gray knit hat. She looked as fearful and apologetic as she had during the days when her daughter Kate was carried off by that crazy insurance man and Agatha had helped rescue her. It was the look of a woman who didn't need any more trouble from the world. Agatha had seen it before, lots of times, on the faces of lots of women.

"Come in, Lydia. I'm glad to see you. I was just thinking that no one has knocked at this door since the first of the year, when Sandy and Kate brought me the cat." It had been a New Year's present, the two girls said, a big wooden cat Sandy had cut out in shop and Kate had colored with Magic Markers.

What did Lydia want? This wasn't a social call, Agatha was certain. She hoped Kate hadn't run off again. Two runaways and a kidnapping should last Kate and her family a lifetime. She and her sister, Sandy, had both seemed pretty happy on New Year's. She remembered that when they left, she had gone straight to her new calendar to turn the months ahead to December and write in big letters, "Christmas presents for Sandy and Kate." Now, as she held the door open for Lydia, she made a mental note to add Lydia's name to her Christmas list.

2

Lydia put three spoonfuls of sugar and a touch of milk in her tea. She stirred it and took a sip before she spoke. "I don't like to bother you again, Agatha. The fact is, you're the only one in Wingate I know well enough to come to. There's my sister Peggy over in Winthrop, but I don't want to ask her. She never did like Ralph. I called in sick this morning to come talk to you."

The name rattled around in Agatha's head before it settled down. Ralph, Ralph. That was the girls' father, Lydia's husband, who lived, she remembered, in Henderson. What had Malcolm Torbert told her, that he was a drunken ne'er-do-well? Something like that.

"If I can help you in any way, Lydia, I certainly will. I'm not doing anything except cutting back raspberry canes, and I won't be able to do that for a while. Look at these hands. I must have a score of thorns in my fingers. They pushed right through the leather gloves Arthur Harper said I should wear. Look!" She held out a hand.

"The girls always have something sticking in their

hands," Lydia said. "If you have some tweezers, I'll take them out for you."

As she went to the bathroom cabinet, it struck Agatha that these were the first decisive words she had ever heard Lydia say. They told her that Lydia knew how to be a mother. It was the outside world she seemed to feel uneasy with.

Now Lydia bent over Agatha's fingers. Apparently she could see the thorns better than Agatha could. "I think that's all of them, Agatha," she said, handing back the tweezers.

"Thank you so much. I'll send you a pailful of berries if they ever come up."

"Don't you bother. I'll send one of the girls to pick them. I've always liked raspberries. We had a patch out back of the house in Albany where I grew up. Call the girls when they're ripe."

That didn't sound right. It was all coming back now. One of the problems during Kate's disappearance was that the Prescotts couldn't afford a phone in their mobile home. Agatha had brought Lydia and Sandy to her own cottage to be near a phone while the police were searching for Kate.

"You have a phone now, do you, Lydia? That's nice for the girls. They won't be so lonely while you're at work. If there's an emergency, they can get in touch right away."

"I don't know how much longer we'll have it. That's sort of why I'm here. You see, Ralph—that's the girls' dad—had a phone put in right after Kate's disappearance. I guess he felt worried about his kids. One day the telephone man came by and connected it. He left one of those expensive

7

Princess phones with buttons and a light. Pink it is, Kate's favorite color. We never saw the bills. Ralph must have had them sent to him—until last week."

"You mean, they took the phone away?" Agatha asked.

"No, the phone's still there. I reckon I can pay for it now. I couldn't a while back. No, it's Ralph who's gone. He drowned in the Winicook two weeks ago; they think he fell off the bridge. The girls and I and his mother from the nursing home buried him in his family plot last week."

Lydia's disclosure, unemotional though it was, called for some expression of sorrow. "I'm so sorry," Agatha said. "I hadn't heard."

"I'm sorry, too, mostly for the girls, if the truth be known. Ralph made life a hell for the three of us, I can tell you. I can't get myself back through all those bad years to remember the couple of good ones we had together. He was drunk, of course. That's what the police said."

"How are Kate and Sandy taking it?"

"Badly, I'm afraid. You see, after Ralph had the phone put in, he called them up more or less regularly. And he started sending little presents, a furry animal or Magic Markers for Kate, some inexpensive jewelry for Sandy. At Christmastime, the presents poured in. Clothes, running shoes—even the right size—an expensive radio–tape player for each girl, and two gift certificates for new bikes at the sporting-goods store over in the mall. They're going to use them as soon as spring comes."

"Do you think he wanted to get back together, Lydia, and was working on the girls?"

"I don't know. He never asked to talk to me. Things are pretty bitter between us. I used to be what they call an

8

abused woman, Agatha." She laughed nervously. "I'm not apt to forget what he did. I would never trust him again." Now, as she asked the questions, Agatha realized police routine was taking over. Once a cop, always a cop. "You have no idea what he was up to?"

"Oh, I suppose he was lonely and had some money left over from his drinking. Ralph wasn't all bad, Agatha. He loved his kids most of the time. The funny thing is, Sandy and Kate maintain he was sober when he talked to them. He was serious, they say, and really concerned about their welfare. They're convinced he was 'normal,' as you might say. That's part of the problem. It would have been different if he had just fallen in the river and drowned without ever checking in. They would have been hurt, but you know how kids bounce back. After three years of not hearing from him and lots of bad memories before that, Ralph wouldn't have been so important. I wish he had left them be."

"They didn't say anything about their father," Agatha told Lydia, "when they brought me that lovely New Year's cat." She pointed to the wooden cat resting on the hearth. "It looks just like Tom."

"They worked hard on it. I think they felt bad they didn't come by more often. Mostly, they ran home to wait for their dad to call."

"He called every day?" Agatha asked. She was surprised. No wonder the girls were upset.

"Not every day. In patches of days, you could say. He wouldn't call for a week or so, then he'd call, apparently, four or five days straight. Always on days when he knew I was at work. Ralph didn't want to talk to me. I'll be honest with you, Agatha. After a while that began to hurt. I felt that he was cutting my children away from me. But I didn't say anything. It was more important for them to have someone else love them too."

"I can understand that, Lydia. This kind of thing happens frequently, if that's any consolation to you."

"And what about the insurance policy?" Lydia asked angrily. "What was he up to there, some sort of final revenge on all of us?"

"What insurance policy?" At last Agatha understood the motive for Lydia Prescott's appearance at her door.

"I'm sorry. I'm getting angry. I have no right to be. Ralph probably meant it for the best. A few weeks ago, in the middle of March, Sandy and Kate received a large envelope in the mail, one of those brown envelopes. It was an insurance policy. The beneficiaries were the girls, not me. Ralph attached a note to the effect that it would take care of their college if something happened. Something happened, all right."

"The girls are taken care of, then? That must be a load off your mind," Agatha commented.

"You would think so, wouldn't you?" Lydia said. "But that's not how it works with people like Ralph. Things just don't work out the way they should."

"The insurance company isn't paying off?"

"How did you know?"

"In accident cases they usually wait to be sure about what happened. Everything has to be in order. They'll pay sooner or later, long before you start thinking about college for Sandy."

"That's exactly what they said, Agatha, almost word for word, when I called the agent. They said since the sum in question was so substantial and the policy so new they had to be sure Ralph's death was an accident. They'll be in touch, the agent said."

"What was the coverage, Lydia?"

Slowly, syllable by syllable, as if she couldn't believe the sounds she was uttering, Lydia pronounced, "Three hundred thousand dollars."

3

Agatha Bates was astonished. She tried to do some quick arithmetic in her head. "How old was Ralph?" she asked.

"Forty," Lydia Prescott told her. "He was twenty-five when we got married." She began to reminisce. Agatha stopped her calculations to listen. Lydia said she was twenty-two, already a waitress, when they married. It was in the City Line Café that she met Ralph Prescott, a fast-talking salesman in the Chevrolet agency. A real sweetheart then, Lydia remembered. The children came along, Lydia quit her job, Ralph started drinking seriously. Agatha knew the rest. Life caught up fast with Ralph and Lydia. They went from a big apartment to a smaller apartment to two rooms and a shared bath. Ralph went from the agency to a used-car lot to selling aluminum windows to a fender shop to nothing. Years of abuse and violence and anger followed, until Lydia at last gathered up her courage and her girls and fled. She didn't bother about a divorce. That didn't matter. She was free. The best thing she could say for Ralph Prescott was that he didn't follow them. Lydia and the girls were lucky, Agatha thought, that they all were still alive. She went back to her arithmetic.

"Your husband must have had to pay a lot in premiums for that amount of coverage," Agatha said. "Did he say anything to Sandy and Kate about a new job? He must have been doing well at something."

"I honestly don't know. I didn't ask them any questions. The fact is, I didn't care what he was doing. I'm sure they heard things they never told me. They knew how it was between Ralph and me, and they tried to stay out of it." Lydia put her hands to her face and broke into sobs. "Why couldn't he leave us be? We were getting along all right. The girls were forgetting him. Why did he have to come back into our lives?"

There was nothing Agatha Bates could say to that, and there was little comfort she could offer the distraught Lydia. Tom was scratching at the back door. He had caught a field mouse, Agatha saw as she went to let him in. It was still alive. "Drop it, Tom," she ordered. The mouse scrambled to the end of the porch and disappeared. Tom followed her into the kitchen to see what she would put in his dish.

When Agatha returned to the living room, Lydia had her coat on and was pulling her knit cap down over her ears. "I'm sorry for the tears. I just had to have someone to talk to. I'll be on my way home now."

"You must come back," Agatha said. "It's important for you and the girls to have someone to talk to now. Or use your phone. Is it all right with you if I go over to the school when it gets out and bring the girls here? I'll see what Arthur Harper next door has to say. He's a lawyer. I'll ask

Chief Torbert if he can find out any more about the accident."

"It would be nice if you brought Sandy and Kate here. They really like you. I don't care about the insurance money, Agatha. It's all right if it doesn't come through. All I care about is my children. We never had much money. We've learned to live without it."

Agatha assured her that was a healthy attitude and offered her a ride. Lydia refused. "It's better if I walk it off. Thanks again, Agatha."

Agatha decided to walk along the road to the school rather than go across the playing field, which had turned to spongy mud in the early spring. She took her boots from the fireplace and put them on. Their warmth felt good. I'm getting along in years, she told herself, when warm soup and warm boots begin to matter.

Arthur Harper was snapping fallen maple branches into pieces to use as kindling. Agatha paused to ask him what he knew about insurance cases. He told her what she already suspected. They were generally settled out of court if there was a problem. What about accidental death and suicide? she asked. She briefly recounted Lydia's story.

Arthur whistled. "That's a lot of money, even these days. The policy is bound to have the usual clause to the effect that the company won't pay on suicides during the first couple of years of the policy's life. They're pretty suspicious of accidental deaths when the policy is new. I'd have to have more information, Agatha."

"Are you still practicing, Arthur?"

"Have you seen me do anything except cut grass, rake leaves, and walk to the post office and back since you moved next door? To answer your question, no."

"Would you take the insurance company on for Lydia Prescott if the company refused to pay and you thought she had a case?"

Arthur appeared to give the matter his consideration. "I'm a corporate lawyer, Agatha. At least, I used to be. Hmm. From what you say, the kids will need the money. I guess I could."

"I'll stand for your bill," Agatha said.

"No, no, there's no need. I'll do it on a contingency basis. Ten percent of whatever we collect. It's usually twenty-five to fifty percent. I don't reckon there will be many expenses. It's a question of negotiating with the company, unless they're hard-nosed about it. In that case Mrs. Prescott will have to decide whether she wants to take them to court."

He bent down to snap a maple branch in half and add the pieces to a little pile he had collected. He looked up at Agatha, who was about to walk on. "It's not very likely, I realize, but isn't there another possibility you haven't mentioned, Agatha? You're a police officer, and Mrs. Prescott's husband sounds as though he led a pretty tough life."

Agatha's mind was on what she was going to say to Sandy and Kate. She was only vaguely aware of what Arthur Harper said. "What did you say, Arthur? What other possibility?"

"I shouldn't say this, I suppose, but what if he was pushed off the bridge in a fight? Or thrown off? No one would live long in the cold current of the Winicook."

Agatha's first impulse was to pay no attention. Arthur wasn't a criminal lawyer. "You've been looking at too many television mysteries, Arthur. Are you going to tell me Lydia had a lover who pushed Ralph into the river?"

15

"No. I'm only thinking of a drunken bum who suddenly seems to be well off and sober and sends his kids expensive presents and suddenly—well, more or less suddenly—insures his worthless life for over a quarter of a million dollars. I'm thinking about Ralph Prescott. You, Agatha, are worried about a widow and her two nice kids. You've forgotten your training, Agatha. What should a smart cop be thinking about?"

"This smart cop would be thinking about how she has to get down the road before school gets out. This smart cop might also be thinking she has a highly suspicious and slightly crazy neighbor. You can have my maple branches, too, Arthur, when you run out of your own."

4

What Arthur Harper had said *did* make some sort of sense, Agatha Bates had to admit. Something had happened to change Ralph Prescott for the better or, perhaps, for the worse, if what Lydia said was true: the phone, the presents, the attention, and, above all, the rather extraordinary insurance policy, which no down-and-out drunk would ever have thought of or been able to afford. And the note to the girls that went with it. She would like to see that note from Ralph.

She would let Sandy and Kate talk their way into it, if they would. Some cookies might help. Agatha looked at her watch, then hurried across the road to the general store. An illustrated tin box of fancy English cookies, or biscuits, as they seemed to be called, caught her eye, as well as some Dutch cocoa to go with them. She gasped at their cost and rummaged in her purse for money she knew wasn't there. That was part of her excuse to Mrs. Reed, and the promise to pay tomorrow. That was what general stores in small towns were for, she thought: to charge you

17

too much for things so they could let you pay the next time you came in.

When she came out, she saw Sandy and Kate across the road, walking home. She shouted and waved. They stopped and waved.

Kate was growing up fast, Agatha noticed as she approached. She was two years younger than twelve-year-old Sandy, but now she was only a couple of inches shorter. Both promised to be tall women. She wondered if Ralph Prescott had been a big man. For some reason Agatha had Ralph down in her mind as a small, thin, nasty man. Most of the wife beaters she had come across in her career with the police were small men; some of them, she was certain, were making up for their size by being tough with their women.

Sandy and Kate smiled a greeting. "Come along with me," Agatha said briskly. "Your mother said I could bring you to my place and stuff you with cookies and cocoa in front of the fireplace."

The girls looked at each other. They both shrugged at the same time. "Okay, I guess," Sandy said. "What about your program, Kate?"

"I don't care if I miss it."

"Are you still watching that soap opera about college kids?" Agatha asked. "What is it called?"

"'College Town,'" Kate replied. "It's still running, but I don't watch it all the time anymore. I'd rather read than watch television." She fell silent and trudged along with Sandy, a couple of steps in back of Agatha.

Tom jumped into Sandy's lap as soon as she sat down. He started to purr and held his head up to be scratched behind his ears.

"He remembers you, Sandy," Agatha said. "Warm yourself by the fire. I'll make the cocoa. Kate, you come along and open the cookies and put some on a plate. It's a lovely box, isn't it? Perhaps you'd like to have it when the cookies are gone."

When they were seated in front of the fire, Agatha asked them how they had been. They answered quietly that they had been all right. Agatha stood up and took away the screen to poke at the smoldering logs. "It doesn't draw this time of year. The air is too heavy. It's about time to clean the ashes out and wait until next fall." She put the screen back and turned to the girls. "I was very sorry to hear about your dad."

Silence. They nibbled on their cookies, sipped their cocoa, and stared into the meager fire. That's almost exactly what I did when Henry died, Agatha realized, except I didn't have any English cookies and Dutch cocoa. I moved up here and stared into a fire that wouldn't burn.

It was Sandy and Kate who had finally brought her out of it last fall. She recalled the day when Sandy, upset and half afraid, had come into the house, sent here by Chief of Police Malcolm Torbert, to tell her Kate was missing.

Straightaway Agatha had gone into action, if you could call it that, and since that day she had been able to live with herself in a reasonable acceptance of her loneliness. She might as well tell Sandy and Kate that. They were old enough to understand.

"I was thinking, after your mother left," she began, "that it's a little over a year ago that my Henry died and I moved up from Boston for good. I wasn't getting along so well until you showed up last September, Sandy, and gave me some interest in the world outside this room. I've

19

been fine since then. I feel that I owe you two something. I had to accept the fact that there was nothing I could do about Henry. He was gone. There's nothing you can do about your father now except grieve. Life goes on. It's easy to say, I know, and harder to do. Do you know what pulled me out of my self-pity? Talking. To my children when they came, to Malcolm Torbert, to the Harpers next door, and most of all, to you, Sandy, and to your mother. I shared your problems then and I'd like to share them now."

"We were on our way to see you, anyway," Kate said defensively. "Maybe tomorrow or Sunday, weren't we, Sandy?"

"Yes. We wanted to ask you to do something for us. We were afraid it would sound sort of crazy."

"There's not much that can sound crazy to a retired police officer. I think I had seen it all by the time I left the force."

"We have to ask Mom first," Kate said.

"Ask her what?" Agatha wanted to know.

"If you could take us to Henderson, to the place where Dad lived. Our aunt took Mom the day after the police called, and the next time she went to make the arrangements. We didn't go."

"We want to see where he lived, Agatha," said Sandy. "It sounds crazy, but we have to see it once, Dad told us so much about it. It's some rooms in a big old factory. Mom said it wasn't much, mostly empty rooms. I don't think she wants to go back, and Aunt Peggy certainly doesn't. She didn't like Dad."

"That sounds normal enough to me, Sandy," Agatha commented. "I'd be glad to take you. Can we get in?"

"Mom has the keys. She said Dad paid the rent a year in advance."

Lydia hadn't mentioned that bit of news to Agatha. She was angry, Agatha thought. She had to be angry. Ralph had come into some money and he wasn't sharing it. Agatha knew from talking to Lydia last fall that she had never asked Ralph Prescott for a penny, but she must have thought in recent months that Ralph ought to help out with more than presents and a pink Princess phone. But she hadn't blamed him for that to Agatha. And she'd said nothing about a year's lease on some rooms in a factory. Did she forget or was she defending her husband because deep down she still loved him?

"More cocoa?" she asked the girls. She took the pot from the hearth and filled both cups. "When did your father move into the factory?"

"Last fall, I guess," Sandy said. "He used to tell us how big it was. It wasn't like an apartment building. You could roller-skate down the corridors. There were some shops and studios and apartments. The rest was empty space they were trying to rent. It was right along the river, next to the bridge."

Now we're getting there, Agatha said to herself. "The same bridge your dad fell from?" she asked.

Kate nodded. "We don't think he fell. How can you fall off a bridge? They have railings along the edge."

"What do you think happened, Kate?"

Kate shrugged her shoulders again and glanced across the hearth at Sandy, who said, "We sort of think Dad jumped into the river and killed himself. We think he tried to make it up to us for being so mean to Mom and us when we lived in Henderson. He took out this insurance policy so we'd be all right the rest of our lives. We don't think he fell. Mom does, but we don't. We think he couldn't live with himself anymore." Sandy's eyes filled with tears.

"Has your mother talked to you about the insurance?"

"Just that it will take a while before they send it to us."

So Lydia did not want—or dare—to disillusion the girls. Agatha wondered if that were her job now. "Tomorrow or Sunday," she suggested, "why don't we drive over to Henderson in the morning, if it's all right with your mother? If she wants to go, too, we'll wait until one of her days off. When are those, Sandy?"

"Sunday and Monday," Sandy said. "But she won't want to go. She looked around the place and said there was nothing there for us. She's going to call the janitor and tell him to clean it out."

5

Agatha decided she had better find out what she could about Ralph Prescott's death before she saw Sandy and Kate again. Clearly Lydia Prescott had not wanted to learn the particulars. Agatha assumed the police in Henderson did not go into any details Lydia did not ask for.

Malcolm Torbert could find out, Agatha was sure. She slipped into her boots and jacket. Tom followed her out the door. He sat on the stoop and licked his paws, watching her head down the road.

The burly chief of police was sitting at his desk cleaning his gun. He stood up to welcome her. "I haven't seen you in a long time, Agatha. Are you bringing me some business?"

Agatha pointed to the pistol parts scattered on his desk. "Did you ever fire that, Malcolm?"

"Once," he admitted. "Charlie Higgins hit a deer in his pickup on Old Winthrop Road. I put it out of its misery. How about you? There are a lot more nasty people down in Boston than we have around here."

Agatha shook her head. She had taken her gun from its holster a number of times and pointed it, but she had never fired it, except in target practice. That was one aspect of her job she had been glad to leave behind when she retired.

"What brings you here?" Torbert asked again. "It's not a social call. You've already made your trip to the center for the day. I saw you walking down the road with the Prescott kids."

"You know about their father?"

"Yes. I gather it was no great loss, and there were no mourners at the funeral. Is Lydia taking it hard?"

"No, but Sandy and Kate are. Did you ever meet Ralph Prescott? Did he ever check in when Kate ran off those two times?"

"I never did, and he never did. I hear he wasn't in any condition to. My friends in Henderson said he stayed drunk. He had a room in a run-down boardinghouse; they took him there when he passed out."

"What did he live on, do you suppose? Lydia said he couldn't keep a job."

"Shoveling snow, delivering advertising handouts, odd jobs like that. Isn't that what the derelicts live on in Boston?"

"One-day jobs at the labor pool and begging. They can eat and sleep at the shelters." Agatha remembered the men along Tremont Street, lining up in front of the liquor store before eight o'clock. Ralph Prescott had not become, it appeared, one of those helpless human beings.

"What's the matter, Agatha?" Torbert asked kindly. "Are you feeling sorry for Lydia and the girls?"

"I don't know. I honestly don't know. I have a feeling there's something wrong. What has happened isn't very

24

clear; at least it's not clear to me. That's really why I'm here, Malcolm."

Agatha went on to tell him briefly about Lydia's visit and her talk with Sandy and Kate.

"These winos never kill themselves, do they?" Torbert asked. "But Kate's right, of course. It's pretty hard to fall off a bridge unless you want to."

"Then there's the insurance."

"Insurance," Torbert exclaimed. "Don't tell me Prescott was insured."

"He was. A couple of weeks before he died he insured himself for three hundred thousand dollars. I'm sorry, I left that out. Arthur Harper says he will help deal with the company. And Arthur said something else I didn't pay any attention to at first. Now I'm puzzling it over. Let me try it out on you, Malcolm." Agatha recounted Arthur's suspicions about Ralph Prescott's sudden change in circumstances and the insurance policy, and Lydia's description of the note to the girls.

"Let me get this straight, Agatha. Ralph Prescott, a well-known alcoholic, may have taken the cure for reasons presently unknown. He made or received some money, something he apparently had had none of for a good long time. He made friends with his two kids and sent them expensive presents. He insured himself for a lot of money and proceeded to die in an accident shortly thereafter."

"And he lived in an old textile mill beside the river."

"Yes, and the police reported to Lydia that he was drunk again when he drowned."

"That's what she says. Was he drunk or did Lydia jump to conclusions or did the police just say he was drunk because that's how they knew him and assumed that's why he

25

ended up in the Winicook River? How was he dressed, like a bum or like someone with money in his pocket? Lydia didn't say and it didn't occur to me to ask and I'd rather not ask her now. She wants it all to go away again. Is it possible, I keep asking myself, that our man Ralph Prescott got into some crooked business and, well, as Arthur suggested, was helped into the river? That doesn't sound likely, does it? Still, the possibility is beginning to bother me. It certainly isn't an idea the insurance people will pursue."

Torbert pulled out a desk drawer to rest his big feet on. He forgot about putting the pistol together. He leaned back in his chair and stared at the ceiling. "Well," he said finally, "you have more information than I do, although it's not much. All I can say is that it sounds kind of strange."

"And . . . ?"

"And you want me to find out some things Lydia didn't ask about, is that right, Agatha? You didn't drop by to talk about service pistols. Okay, I'll give Melankamp a call. He was the officer in Henderson I was in touch with the two times Kate took off. He knew Prescott. I'll drop by on my way home, Agatha, unless I can't reach Melankamp. In that case, I'll give you a ring."

The talk with the chief hadn't been altogether satisfying, but it would have to do. Malcolm didn't have many mysteries in Wingate to test his wits. Agatha went home to study the contents of the freezer: frozen chicken pie, frozen beef pie, frozen minute steaks that always melted into a gray mush before they were done, frozen lasagna, and frozen shrimp curry. She sighed. She had been a disappointment to Henry, who believed in good food cooked well. Clam chowder was nourishing. Tom was fond of chowder, too. He would take care of what was left over.

There were two phone calls at the end of her busiest day since Christmas, two phone calls and a visit. Sandy phoned to say they could go to Henderson the next day if that was all right with Agatha. Lydia didn't want to go. Sandy would have the keys and the directions. Malcolm Torbert called to tell her not to go away. He would be by in a few minutes. Agatha wondered where Malcolm thought she would be going.

"I called Fred Melankamp," Torbert began soon after he arrived at Lydia's house. "He only knew that Prescott ended up in the Winicook. He promised to talk to Paul Trudeau, the officer on the case. He just called back. He caught Trudeau before he went off duty. I'm here to tell you what he said, Agatha, and ask if you have a can of cold beer. It's been a long day."

"You're worn out from cleaning your gun and school-bus duty, are you, Malcolm? I'm sorry, I don't have any beer. Will sherry do?"

Torbert made a face. "It won't do, but it will have to do." He went to the fire and did some things to it that Agatha never managed to do right. The flames flared up from the charred logs. "You must keep the ashes from piling up under the logs, Agatha. The fire has to breathe in this kind of weather or the logs will just sit there and smolder."

He took a swallow of sherry and grimaced. He rolled the glass between his hands to warm it, then set it down and studied a scrap of paper he pulled from his pocket.

"Let's see now. Ralph Prescott went into the Winicook

27

River, one way or another, on March thirtieth, about nine o'clock in the evening, presumably from the Twin City Bridge. It was raining that night. He was seen by a patrol officer leaning against the railing at the east end of the bridge a little before nine. The officer knew Ralph and waved. Prescott waved back. He wasn't there thirty minutes later when the patrol car came back. His body was sighted the next morning about a hundred yards downstream, lodged between some rocks. They think the current carried him downstream. That much the police know or have good reason to suppose.

"Technically, he may not have fallen from the bridge. Trudeau doesn't remember exactly what he said to Lydia when she came. He's a French Canadian by birth and his English, Fred says, is good, but not perfect. He does remember that Lydia asked him very few questions. Mostly she listened. What Trudeau thinks might have happened is that Prescott slipped down the bank into the water and got swept under by the current. The river is high this year from all the melting snow up-country. It's running well above its normal level. It's very dangerous. They have had to pull a kid out already this spring, Fred told me. Anyway, at the end of the bridge, just beyond the railing, there's a path down the bank. People use it to go down and fish from the rocks in the summer. It was pretty slippery that night, and if Ralph was drunk, he might have lost his footing and rolled down into the river and that was that. Trudeau thinks that's what happened."

"Or he jumped?" Agatha asked.

"Maybe," Torbert said. "They think not, but they couldn't be sure. He did wave to the patrol car. Anyway,

Ralph was pretty scraped up when they brought him ashore. They *are* certain he drowned."

"What about being drunk?"

"I asked Fred that. He wasn't legally drunk according to the blood test, but there was alcohol in his system. To the police in Henderson, Ralph Prescott was a wino. That's how they saw him."

"He wasn't staggering when the patrol officer saw him?" Agatha asked.

"He wasn't moving at all. He was leaning with his back against the railing. And he waved."

"That doesn't sound like someone who's going to take his life. It almost sounds as though he was out for a walk or waiting for someone. What was he wearing?"

"Nothing out of the ordinary, except Trudeau believes the clothes were sort of new. Expensive boots, wool socks, heavy cotton pants, T-shirt, wool shirt, and expensive jacket. Nothing much in his pockets, handkerchief and a wallet with his social security card and driver's license and a few dollars."

"Nothing else? That seems odd to me. Keys?"

"Not on him. They were on a chair in what he used as his bedroom, a room with a mattress on the floor in the old mill. Nothing much in the rooms, Fred says. Everything is still there."

"No one paid much attention to his passing, would you say, Malcolm?"

"Trudeau apparently didn't. Why should he? What did you do when you found a wino frozen on a Boston sidewalk?"

"We sent him to the morgue and tried to find out who he

was so we could notify the next of kin. You're right, Malcolm. The police did their job. They knew Ralph Prescott. He was the local drunk. Lydia didn't cause them any problems. What happened must have seemed natural enough to her. She took Ralph off to his family plot and buried him. That was that. Except for the insurance policy."

"I was getting to that," Chief Torbert said. "An investigator from the company came around to talk to Trudeau and the coroner. He got them to admit Prescott *could* have taken a dive. They had to agree there was nothing to prove he didn't. And, I didn't know this, right after Lydia left with the daughters three years ago, Prescott turned on the gas in the kitchen and put his head in the oven. He forgot to close the door and windows. He was in the hospital for a day or two. That seemed to please the investigator. He hasn't been back."

"Arthur should know that if he decides to take on the company. What about mud on his clothes if he slipped down the path? No one checked into that?"

"Fred didn't say. It would have been washed out anyway, wouldn't it? Lydia must have his clothes. Are you going to ask her, Agatha? You said she wanted to forget him."

"I'll see. It sounds as though the police in Henderson have the right answer, but the insurance people have enough to challenge them. Lydia will have to decide whether to pursue it. She may not care about the money now, but she will someday. So will Sandy and Kate. I'll have a talk with Arthur."

"That's it, then, Agatha." Torbert drained the sherry and made another face.

"Thank you so much, Malcolm. Drop by more often. I'll keep a can of beer in the refrigerator for you." She paused. "One thing. Would it be all right if I used your name in case I want to talk to Fred Melankamp?"

"Going back to work, are you, Agatha? Once a cop, always a cop, like they say. Be my guest."

How long has it been since I've been here? Agatha asked herself, as she poked the Toyota into the outskirts of Henderson. Certainly a long time. When they spent their summers in Wingate, there wasn't much reason to go to Henderson. She and Henry brought what they needed from Boston or went over to the mall between Wingate and the city. The last time they were here, she recalled, was when they came looking for a cycle shop that had the kind of bicycle their daughter Sarah wanted for her birthday. Henry got lost, then confused, and finally furious before they found the shop on a little street north of town. After that, they stuck with the mall.

Henderson was divided in two by the Winicook River, which had once supplied the power for the great textile mills stretched along its east bank; that much she knew. When she mentioned this to Sandy, who sat in the front seat by agreement with Kate, who would ride there on the return trip, Sandy said she already knew that. She had done a sixth-grade report about the mills for social studies. She told Agatha and Kate that Henderson had been one of the principal mill towns in New England. "It wasn't so great when we lived there, was it, Kate?" she concluded.

"I don't remember much of anything, except playing on the sidewalks and how hot our room was in the summer. And it was a long walk to school, just like it is in Wingate."

As they approached the bridge, Agatha noticed ahead of them on the right an overhanging sign for the City Line Café. "Look," she said without thinking, "there's the restaurant your mother used to work at before you two were born." As soon as the words were out of her mouth, Agatha regretted them. That was Lydia's business, not hers.

"Where?" Sandy and Kate said at once.

Agatha pulled in to the curb in front of the café, which looked as though it had been there a long time. Age had not improved its appearance. A beer sign flashed in a window that had not been washed in a long time.

"It doesn't look like much," Sandy said.

"I think most of the business in town has moved across the river, and the City Line was left behind."

"Mom worked here?" Kate asked.

Agatha told them what their mother had told her. The girls latched on to the fact that their mother and father had met there. It seemed important to them.

"Do you think we could have lunch here?" Sandy asked. "It doesn't look so hot, but I'd sort of like to, and Kate would, too. I brought some money Dad sent us. We can pay."

"I suppose so," Agatha said. "Lots of times these places are better inside than they are outside. When I was a police officer, the best places we ate at in our district were called greasy spoons and they looked like this."

The money . . . Lydia hadn't mentioned that. "It was nice of your dad to send you some money," she said cautiously. "Still, I'd prefer to take care of lunch, if I may. Save your money for your mother's birthday."

"That's what it was for, anyway, Sandy," Kate said. "You shouldn't have brought it." She leaned forward to explain to Agatha that Ralph Prescott had sent them two one-hundred-dollar bills to buy their mother something for Christmas and for her birthday. There wasn't much for them to buy at the general store, so they still had most of the money left. "Mom's birthday is in May," Kate said. "We'll buy her something really nice and tell her it's from Dad."

"Maybe we will and maybe we won't, Kate," Sandy commented. "We'll wait and see. Dad didn't say it had to be from him."

"Yeah, but he won't be sending any more, will he, Sandy? Mom ought to have one good thing she knows is from him. What do you think, Agatha?"

"I think I should drive you to the mall whenever you want to go. I'll be glad to discuss it with you then. Right now, let's find the mill."

Agatha asked the girls if they remembered the bridge they were crossing.

"Is this the Twin City Bridge?" Sandy asked. She didn't ask whether this was the bridge where Ralph Prescott had taken his life.

"Yes, and there's the mill your father lived in, I think," Agatha replied, nodding ahead to a long brick building. At the far end, garish signs announced discount wares and space for rent. The near end of the building was desolate. It looked empty behind the broken windows. Agatha drove to the parking lot at the end of the occupied half. She was surprised to find it half filled.

On the first floor was a series of shops off a wide corridor, most of them selling discount sweaters and shoes and cheap clothing. An arrow pointed up a flight of stairs. A handmade sign told them they could find studios, apartments, and the rental office.

Another flight of stairs led to a third floor. The office was on the second floor. A young man in paint-splattered jeans and shirt was sitting on the desk inside, tacking a piece of heavy canvas to a square frame. "What can I do for you?" he asked.

Agatha introduced the Prescott children. "We'd like to see Ralph Prescott's apartment, please. Sandy has the key."

"Sure, come along. It's down at the end at the brick divide. I'm sorry about your dad," the man said to Kate and Sandy. "He used to come into my studio to talk. Right in there." He pointed to a door they passed. "I get it free for keeping track of things on the second floor. The manager looks after the first floor. So far, there's nothing on the third floor."

"How many people live here, Mr., um. . .," Agatha asked.

"I'm sorry. I'm Don Ostel. Well, it all depends. Nobody lives here in the winter except occasionally. It's too cold. We have only three regular apartments, if that's what you call them. The rest are studios or storage rooms. Mr. Prescott was the only real tenant. The artists often sleep in their studios in the warmer months."

"Dad was the only man here at night?" Sandy asked. "That's scary."

"Sometimes people work late. There's a night watchman who comes around a couple of times. He's from the next mill down the river. Here's your dad's place."

As Sandy fitted the key into the lock, Agatha looked back toward the stairs. The door was two hundred feet, at least, from the stairs; probably a lot more. The reborn Ralph Prescott had come to a lonely place. Why was that? If he was well off, as he seemed to be, he didn't have to live here.

Sandy got the door open. Lydia had described the apartment accurately. It was three almost-empty rooms. Really, it was only open space divided by flimsy partitions: a big room you walked into, which had a worktable in the middle and a hot plate and a refrigerator on a smaller table in one corner; a smaller room with a toilet and basin and shower in a corner behind a curtain; and a third room that had a mattress on the floor, blankets and a pillow piled nearby, an expensive lounge chair, a large electric heater, and a hanging clothes pole against the wall. This was not a place, Agatha thought, where one lived; it was only a place where one stayed.

"This is it," Ostel said. "The police came by once and brought Mrs. Prescott and her sister by later on." He noticed the girls' disappointment. "I'm sorry there's not more here for you. Would you like to come down to my studio and have some cocoa before you leave? I'll show you my work."

"Why don't you do that?" Agatha suggested. "I'll be back in a little while. I'd like to poke around outside."

Sandy started to speak, but stopped. Agatha could see

36

she had no desire to go to the bridge. "Okay," she agreed. "Kate and I will wait for you."

Agatha made the long walk back to the stairwell, trying to imagine the bustle and noise of the mill when it was working. All of this enormous space, three long floors of space, had been filled with activity. Now the machinery was gone and the space was partitioned into studios and shops. Someday, she assumed, the lonely hulk would be filled from one end to the other with apartments or condominiums and quaint little shops.

She walked across the parking lot and the highway to the bridge. The river must have receded. Logs, boxes, plastic containers, and tires marked the line on the bank where the high water had reached. Rocks broke the surface of the sweeping current. Even now, no one would last long in the cold waters of the Winicook.

At the end of the bridge, where the pavement turned right along the highway, Agatha found the path down the slope, just as Officer Melankamp had described it to Malcolm Torbert. Today, in the sunlight, it didn't look treacherous. But it was not hard to imagine someone slipping and sliding down the muddy slope on a dark, rainy night.

Agatha walked onto the bridge. She stopped about fifty paces from the end and leaned back against the railing. She shook the railing. It was firmly anchored. She measured it with her eye. It was at least five feet high. Trudeau was right. It wasn't a railing you would fall over by accident, drunk or sober.

She walked slowly back to the path. It came right up to the pavement where the railing ended. Ten or twelve feet from the sidewalk, it pitched sharply down. It would take more than a stagger or two to carry you from the sidewalk to the slope, Agatha realized. She wondered if Ralph Prescott had, for reasons known to himself, started down the path that night and slipped. He must have been aware of its danger. No, Agatha was as certain that Ralph Prescott hadn't slipped down the bank as she was that he hadn't climbed over the railing and dropped into the river. Perhaps Officer Trudeau had come to his conclusion too quickly.

But why shouldn't he have? Agatha argued with herself. Who but a drunk would be leaning against a bridge railing on a cold, rainy night? Who but a drunk would have been so careless of his safety that he took a small shortcut from one pavement to another? If you saw Ralph Prescott the way Trudeau must have seen him, staggering along the city's sidewalks for years, it was easy to believe that was what happened.

Then how to explain his new boots, his apparently sensible and expensive clothing, personal possessions no real drunk would pay attention to? Arthur Harper's remarks impressed themselves deeper into Agatha's consciousness. Ralph Prescott might have gone down the path to the river by accident or by intent. On the other hand, he might have had some "help."

7

"Shall we take a last look at the apartment before we leave?" Agatha asked Sandy and Kate, who were seated on a cot, listening to Don Ostel explain his art. "I have to use latex house paint," he explained. "I can't afford good oils. That's probably why I do abstract stuff. It's easier."

His paintings were compositions of blaring reds, yellows, greens, and oranges, splashed across the canvas. Agatha had to respect the strength and colors. Beyond that, she wasn't sure.

"Lock the door when you leave," the artist told Sandy. "If your mother wants me to clean it out, she has my number. There's not much, is there? If she doesn't want them, I'll take the chair and the heater and the little refrigerator. No hurry. The place is paid for until November."

"The lease runs from November first of last year, then?" Agatha asked. "Is that when Ralph Prescott moved in?"

"That's right. He was using the place off and on for a month before that. Then he took out a year's lease."

39

"What was he using the place for, do you know?" she asked.

"Not really. I saw him moving boxes in and out once in a while."

"Cartons?"

"Coming in, yes. Going out, smaller boxes. There are a couple on his worktable. I didn't pay much attention. He put that heavy lock on the door. This is a creepy place at night."

"I see," Agatha said. Maybe she would have a talk with Ostel later. And with Melankamp and Trudeau. But what about the life-insurance policy? She decided that was Lydia's business.

"There's nothing here you two want?" she asked when they were once again in Ralph Prescott's bleak apartment.

"There's nothing here," Kate said. She looked inside the refrigerator, which was empty. "What we wanted, I guess, was just a little thing to remind us of Dad. Something personal. It's like he didn't actually live here. Do you think he had another place, Agatha?"

"I'll try to find out for you, Kate. Chief Torbert has a friend on the police force here. I'll talk to him. Maybe we'll come back. How about the clothes?"

"I don't think I could wear any of Dad's things, even if they fit," Sandy remarked. "It wouldn't seem right."

"How big was your father, Sandy?" She could get that straight, at least, Agatha thought. She had no idea what Ralph Prescott looked like.

"He was big," Sandy said proudly. "Mom says Kate and I are going to have some of his size."

"He was more than six feet tall," Kate added. "He used

40

to play football on the high-school team until he quit school."

"Oh," said Agatha. "The clothes certainly wouldn't fit either of you for a while, would they?" She went over to a pole hanging from two wires. Two suits and a tweed jacket and two pairs of tan wool trousers were hanging there. She looked at the labels in the jackets. "You might tell your mother these are expensive suits, Sandy, before she gives them away."

Beneath the hanger were three boxes of neatly folded clothes. "Why don't you look inside the boxes here? There might be something personal tucked under the clothes, since your dad didn't have a bureau to put things in."

As the girls laid clothing on the floor from one of the cartons, Agatha noticed that the shirts and underwear and corduroy trousers were also expensive, if she was any judge of men's apparel. Ralph Prescott had made a complete change of life, that was certain. She went into the large front room to study the several boxes on the worktable. They were strong reinforced mailing boxes of different sizes. There was a nest of tissue paper in each one.

"Agatha!" she heard Kate cry out from the bedroom. "Come quick."

Kate and her sister were kneeling beside the carton. Each of them held a small package wrapped in clowns-and-balloons birthday paper. Agatha knelt beside them. A birthday card with Sandy's name was taped to one package and a card with Kate's name to the other.

They looked at Agatha silently for permission to open their packages. "What do you think?" Sandy finally asked. "It's a long way to our birthdays. Should we wait?"

41

Agatha was as curious as the girls. "What would your mother say?" she asked.

"Mom doesn't really want to hear about Dad," Kate said. "We don't talk about him unless she asks. She wouldn't care, Sandy. It's not like these were presents from Aunt Peggy or our grandmother that come early."

"I suppose it's okay. Dad wouldn't care. Let's."

They stripped off the wrappings. Inside each package was a box similar to the smallest one on the worktable. These, too, were stuffed with tissue paper. Sandy, then Kate, unfolded the paper with excited fingers. In surprise and disappointment, they saw what was inside. Kate held out an object to Agatha. "What's this thing?" she asked.

Agatha took it gently and considered what it was. She was pretty sure it was an ivory carving of a polar bear six or seven inches long. The carving was ridged along the back. The bear's mouth yawned open.

Sandy showed her a curious ivory knife, hunched figures carved along the blade. "A knife?" she asked.

"A knife and a bear, I think. They are probably ivory. I have a suspicion they are very old, but no idea how old. I think they are Eskimo; I can't be sure. I'm only a police officer."

"We could ask Don. He might know," Sandy said.

"Let's wait a bit," Agatha told her. "We'll find someone who can really help us. Wrap them up carefully. We'll take them with us."

"How valuable, Agatha?" Sandy asked. "As much as a hundred dollars? Are they worth that much, do you think?"

"Much more than that, if they are authentic. Let's go on to lunch."

42

She would have to ask Lydia to hold off cleaning out Ralph's place, she realized. She couldn't believe Ralph Prescott, the high-school dropout, was a collector of antiquuities. A stealer, maybe, but not a buyer.

Sandy and Kate must have had the same opinion. They sat across from Agatha in a booth at the City Line Café and puzzled over the meaning of their birthday presents. "Do they sell stuff like that in a mall, Agatha?" Kate asked.

"I don't think so, Kate."

"Well, where did he get them?" Kate insisted.

Agatha didn't answer directly. "First, we will have to find out what they are and where they come from. That may be hard to do. In the meantime, why don't you order? It's rather pleasant inside, isn't it? Maybe your mother would like to come here with us on one of her days off and have lunch, for old times' sake. She could tell us how it used to be."

Sandy asked what Brunswick stew was. When Agatha told her, she settled for a hamburger and fries. Kate wanted the same, with hot chocolate.

The smell of stale grease from the kitchen did not reassure Agatha. "Apple pie and coffee," she told the waitress.

"You went out to the bridge, didn't you?" Sandy asked.

"I did. Did either of you want to go?"

"No," Sandy answered. "Heights make me dizzy. I don't want to see where Dad jumped."

What to say? The insurance company might never agree, but Agatha was certain that Ralph Prescott had never swung his leg over the railing and let himself drop into the raging Winicook underneath. And he hadn't thrown himself down the slope, either. He was too well off, as Officer Trudeau would have discovered if he had pursued the matter. Prescott was proud of the clothes he had laundered and neatly folded into the cardboard cartons. Slipped? Maybe yes. Pushed? Maybe yes.

"I don't think your dad jumped, Sandy," she said at last.

"But he loved us—he told us that—and he wanted us to be all right," Kate objected. "He was a hero."

"Your dad certainly wanted the best for you both," Agatha explained. "He understood he could help you more if he stayed alive. It was an accident of some sort. When the insurance company finds that out, your mother and you won't have to worry about the future. You know," she went on quickly, determined to set the matter straight, since Lydia didn't want to deal with it, "your dad's insurance wouldn't be good unless it was an accident. That's what Arthur Harper next door told me. He's a lawyer."

"He fell?" Kate asked in a tone of disbelief.

"It would be easy to do at the end of the bridge where there wasn't any railing. It was raining and the slope to the river was slippery."

The girls were silent, chewing their hamburgers and dipping their greasy fries in catsup.

"One thing I'd like to have you tell me," Agatha requested, "is what the note said that came with the insurance policy. Do you remember exactly?"

"Yes," said Sandy. "Dad was teasing us, we thought. 'Just in case something happens to me, I want you and your mother to be looked after. Nothing's going to happen, but you can never tell these days, can you?'"

Arthur Harper was scattering lime over his muddy lawn. "I don't really know," he remarked to Agatha, "if this lime works or not. Some experts say yes; others say it's a waste of money. But I've always done it, so I might as well keep it up."

"I don't think Henry ever bothered," Agatha said. "I don't remember that he ever put anything on the grass out front here."

"You're right, Agatha. Don't think I didn't notice. That's what a good neighbor does: keeps track of the other guy's lawn. And every year, you know, your grass is just as lush and green or just as patchy, depending on the rain, as mine."

"What did you decide about the Prescotts' insurance?" Agatha asked.

"I thought I'd look into it. The policy is with Universal Life, I found out from Malcolm Torbert. From what you said, I didn't want to bother Mrs. Prescott. The district agent lives over in Winthrop. He works in Henderson. He sold Prescott the policy. He said he'll drop by this week-end."

Agatha Bates told him about her trip to Henderson. "Prescott was doing something successful, I am convinced of that. Whether it was legal or not, I can't say. It was certainly private." She went on to describe the apartment in the mill and what Don Ostel had told the girls and her. She did not mention the ivory carvings. They would wait for a talk with Torbert.

"You know the Twin City Bridge, don't you, Arthur? There's a four-to-five-foot iron railing along the sidewalk over the bridge. Chief Torbert found out Prescott was lean-ing against it the night he died, waving to a passing patrol car."

"Drunk?" Arthur asked.

"Perhaps, but not very, it would seem."

Arthur did not know about the sharply dropping path to the rocks and the river. "It was raining, the police say," Agatha continued. "He could have cut across a patch of bare land from the bridge walkway to the sidewalk along the street on his way home. I suppose if he was careless or unsteady, he could have fallen down the bank. The streetlight is a good distance away. It's hard for me to believe he didn't know where he was and even harder to believe he took it in his head to throw himself down a muddy trail hoping he would end up in the Winicook. If he wanted to die, he had to go over the rail."

"The investigator told Webb there was some room for doubt in the police report. Also, Prescott put his head in the oven the day after his family left him."

"Torbert told me."

"Well, there you are. That's all they needed. Universal

46

isn't going to part with three hundred thousand without a fight. Another thing, Prescott paid the two years' premium in advance. That's another tip-off to them. Something like this can drag on forever. I'm sure Webb has lots of arguments and an offer to settle cheap up his sleeve. We'll see what he says."

"And if Prescott was pushed, perhaps in a fight?"

"They would have to pay, of course. Are you going to find out if he was pushed, Agatha? I thought you had retired." He spoke seriously. "There are just as many dangerous people out here in the sticks, Agatha, as there are in the city. And if Prescott was pushed, does that tell you anything?"

"It does," Agatha agreed. "I should stay home and put lime on my grass and watch it grow. Is that it, Arthur?"

"That's it," Arthur grumped. He picked up his bucket of lime and returned to his job.

It *was* good advice, Agatha understood, as she went on down the road to the town hall. She couldn't remember that when Henry was alive people ever told her what not to do. They saved all their advice for widows. She asked herself what she was up to and why. Lydia wanted to forget her husband forever, and as quickly as possible. Kate and particularly Sandy seemed willing, even relieved, to abandon their romantic notions of a father who took his own life for their well-being. They would collect something from Universal if Arthur Harper kept after the company. Why not let it be?

Still, that left the artifacts. What should she do about them? They were meaningless to Sandy and Kate, who had no comprehension of their potential value. But could they ever belong to the girls? Were they Ralph Prescott's to give

47

away? She had her doubts about that. She would see what Torbert had to say, unless it was his day off.

It was not. Deputy Parker MacDonald had this Saturday off. Tomorrow was Torbert's free day. The two of them alternated, Malcolm told Agatha; sometimes they exchanged weekends, sometimes Saturdays and Sundays. What he really needed, the chief complained, was another deputy.

Agatha gave him a complete account of the trip to Henderson. She unwrapped the two pieces of ivory from a scrap of soft flannel; she had kept them when the girls said they'd rather leave them with her since they didn't like them all that much. Maybe Agatha, they said, could find out what they were.

Torbert did not pick them up at first. He twisted the gooseneck lamp to shine down on them. Then he picked up the strange-looking knife by the tip and turned it over. Next he looked inside the polar bear's mouth. "It's stained red inside," he observed. "Do you think he just ate?"

"I think his last meal was hundreds of years ago, Malcolm. What do you think?"

Torbert shrugged and put the carvings down on the desk blotter.

"They were each wrapped up in a box with birthday paper around it, one for Kate and the other for Sandy. The same kind of box Prescott used, if the janitor-artist is right, to carry things out of the factory. Things that may have come into the factory in a larger carton, to be separated out into smaller boxes."

"And what about the boxes he had his clothes in? Were they the same kind he used to bring the stuff into the mill? What did they look like?" Torbert asked.

Agatha felt the blood rush to her face. What a fool I am, she thought. She had been so concerned with the clothes and presents that she had paid no attention to the cartons. Their possible importance had never occurred to her.

She looked sheepishly at Torbert. "I blew it, Malcolm. I can't tell you, because I didn't pay any attention to them. I'm almost certain they were plain." She forced herself to remember. She could not recall any printing or label on the boxes under the clothes pole. The remote smell of apples came back to her. Was that from the clothes or the boxes? It wasn't so strong she noticed it at the time. "No markings, I'm pretty sure. How about apple boxes, Malcolm?"

"They usually have something on them. The ones they use around here aren't all that strong."

"These were sturdy boxes, I do remember that."

Torbert changed the subject. "Is there any question that if someone slipped down the slope there, he'd end up straight in the river? There are rocks, aren't there, that might catch someone before he went in?"

"There are now," Agatha agreed, "but I can't say about the night Prescott died. You can tell from the high-water line that the river was flowing maybe three feet farther up the bank. I think the chances are pretty good the current would have grabbed Prescott."

"But it's possible he could have slipped or been pushed and not gone into the river?"

"I suppose so," Agatha agreed.

"Or, conceivably, he could have fallen and knocked himself silly and gone into the water by mistake?"

"Conceivably."

"But he didn't slip and slide and crawl down there to take an early spring swim?" Torbert asked finally.

"That's not likely, is it?"

"I gathered from Melankamp no one made a great effort to find out. Ralph Prescott wasn't that important, and drunks have accidents all the time. That seems reasonable."

"But there is the insurance, isn't there, Malcolm, and the note that he sent the girls with the policy? It wasn't your ordinary policy and it wasn't your ordinary note. Ralph didn't say, 'If I die' or some such. He said, 'If something happens to me.'"

"Well, Agatha, they are just words. You can't tell now what he meant when he wrote them. What else would he say? Folks don't like to talk about dying. It's always 'If something happens,' isn't it?"

Agatha disagreed. "I can think of several different things he could have written. There was something on his mind, Malcolm, and it wasn't suicide. People who buy a lot of good clothes and start to take care of them don't kill themselves. They look after themselves, too. And these two pieces of ivory on your desk. They are old, and if they are really old, they are valuable. Isn't that so, Malcolm?"

"I don't know rightfully if they are so old," Torbert argued. "They look old, that's for sure. They may be fake. Have you thought of that? Ralph Prescott might have been in the fake antiques business."

"For himself or for someone else?"

"I'm no use to you there, Agatha. But I know who is. Our town eccentric, Dr. Mavis Langhorne."

"I've never heard of her," Agatha said. "Who is she? Why do you say she's eccentric?"

"Dr. Langhorne has a cabin—it's more like a shack—out on the town forest road. She lives there with a couple of giant Newfoundlands. Nice dogs. She walks everywhere, to town, over to the mall when she has to, and all the way to Boston about once a year."

"That doesn't make her an eccentric. What is she a doctor of?"

"Archaeology or anthropology, I can't keep the two apart. Whichever. She was a curator of a museum at a university in Boston, I heard. When they didn't make her director, because she was a woman—or maybe because she was a little eccentric—she quit and moved up to her summer place to live year-round. Sort of like you, Agatha." Torbert laughed. "No offense."

"Are you suggesting that the two crazy women in town get together and leave you be to direct traffic on the Fourth of July, is that it, Malcolm?"

"I didn't mean it that way, Agatha."

"Then what do you mean, Chief Torbert?"

Torbert sighed. "I mean I'm sorry it's not my day off," he muttered.

Agatha headed for the door without a word. It was like in Boston, where it had taken her twenty years to be accepted by the men on the force.

"Agatha," Torbert called after her, "you'll be needing this sooner or later."

Hand on the knob, she turned.

Torbert came around his desk holding a badge. "This makes you a deputy cop in Wingate. We never had a lady deputy in town before."

Agatha took it. "You probably never needed one until now. No offense."

51

9

"Maybe Agatha is right," Sandy said. "Maybe Dad slipped down into the river on his way back to the factory. She said it was raining."

Kate and Sandy sat at the counter eating the doughnuts Mom had left there the night before when she came home from work. Agatha's remarks had disturbed Sandy. She didn't like the idea of her father taking his own life. It made her feel guilty after accepting all the nice things he had done just before that. And she didn't like the idea of his slipping down the bank into the cold Winicook River, either. That meant he was drunk, and she had hoped he had given up drinking.

Agatha hadn't sounded so sure it was an accident, she recalled. She must have meant something even worse had happened to her father. Sandy closed her mind to the possibility. She tried to find something in her memory of Dad that was good. There wasn't much. Most of what she remembered were slaps, shouts, fear, poverty, and tears.

The truth was she had forgotten her father. Like her mother, Sandy's happiness lay in being left alone to lead her own life, such as it was. Then Dad had come back—not actually, but over the phone—and sounded happy talking to Kate and her by turns, telling them what he was going to do as soon as he got some business out of the way. "Don't tell your mother a word of this," he had said to Sandy, not to Kate, "but next summer I'd like to come visit you girls. I'll tell your mother first, but not just yet. I have to be sure of something first."

Sandy had thought her father had to be sure he was through with drinking, but maybe that wasn't it. Anyway, she hadn't told Mom and she hadn't breathed a word to Kate. Kate had a few good memories of Dad, and Sandy didn't want her to be disappointed.

Now they sat at the counter, half expecting the phone to ring, although it never rang on Sunday, because Dad never called on Mom's days off.

Mom hadn't been too happy when Dad put the phone in, but she hadn't stopped him. "You guys are his kids, too," she explained, "and he has a right to talk to you if he wants. Your father was a good man, when he wasn't drinking."

Dad didn't say much about himself. He said he had moved into a big place where they could come and roller-skate someday if it was okay with their mother. He tried to find out what Sandy wanted for Christmas. And how they were both doing at school. That seemed important to him. "You both have to do well in school," he said three or four times. "I dropped out when I shouldn't have. I think my troubles started then, Kate. I didn't feel I was as good as the kids who finished, even when I was making more money for a while than they were. Now I feel okay. I feel pretty good about myself."

Kate hadn't asked why. Sandy said it was Dad's way of telling her he wasn't drinking and had a good job. They agreed he must have had a good job, a better job than Mom's in the restaurant at the Winthrop House. She couldn't afford presents like the ones Dad sent.

"Do you want the last doughnut, Sandy?" she asked.

"You take it, Kate. I don't like cinnamon doughnuts that much. I like powdered sugar better."

"They didn't have any powdered sugar at the Day and Night Store," Lydia said from the hallway. She was in her bathrobe, combing the tangles out of her hair, which was long and sort of curly like Kate's. It was Sandy, she used to say, who had her father's straight, fine hair.

She sat down on the third stool, between the two girls. Sandy went to the other side of the counter to pour her mother a cup of the coffee she had made earlier. She took the orange juice out of the little refrigerator. "Do you want some toast, Mom?" she asked.

"What kind of jelly do we have, Sandy?"

Sandy poked around in the refrigerator. There was the grape that they used for making their school lunch; it was the cheapest jelly the general store had. At the back of the shelf there was a jar of raspberry. She took off the top to see if it was moldy. "Raspberry all right?" she asked.

"Fine." Lydia hugged herself and shivered with pleasure. "I can't tell you two how wonderful Sundays are. There's nothing like being waited on yourself, I can tell you. If only every day were Sunday and the three of us were together like this with nothing to do. Oh, how I wish!"

"How much did you and Aunt Peggy make yesterday?"

54

Kate asked. Her mother and Peggy split their tips. Kate liked to keep track of what her mother made. It was a different amount every time.

"I don't know, honey. I just stuffed it in my purse. I was so tired. Get my purse and we'll see."

Kate spread the money on the counter, separating it into piles of one- and five-dollar bills and another pile for the change. "Hey, Mom," she shouted, "there's a ten-dollar bill here. You don't get them very often."

"That was the party of four from Henderson," Lydia said. "Rich-looking people don't always leave big tips, but the man put down a ten and a five on top of it and said thank you very much when they left. Usually, you only get the tens from a table of eight." Lydia often wondered why, when you stopped to add them up, the tips in the elegant Winthrop House didn't really amount to as much as the working people had left for her in the City Line Café.

"What were you guys talking about?" she asked Sandy, who was waiting for the second piece of toast to pop up.

"Nothing much," Sandy said.

"We were arguing about Dad," Kate piped up. "You have seventy-three dollars here, Mom, plus the change. That's pretty good."

"What about Dad?" Lydia demanded.

"I still say he killed himself," Kate replied. "Now Sandy says she's not so sure. Agatha went out to the bridge and took a look. She doesn't think he jumped over the railing."

Somehow, Lydia Prescott didn't want Agatha Bates butting into her children's lives. Kate and Sandy had enough problems without being confused about Ralph's death. If they wanted to believe their father died like a hero to provide for their future, well, there were worse things to believe. It might take the place of other, uglier remembrances they never talked about.

Lydia said nothing. It was Sandy who picked up Kate's remark. "Agatha thinks Dad slipped down the bank, like you said the policeman told you. And Agatha sort of thinks something else might have happened, but she didn't go into it."

"Like what, Sandy?" Trudeau hadn't mentioned any other possibility to Lydia.

"Like maybe Dad was pushed, I think."

"Mom," Kate interrupted. "Mom, we went to the restaurant where you used to work, the City Line or something. We had lunch there, hamburgers and fries. Agatha said you met Dad there. Is that right, Mom? You never told us you met Dad in a restaurant."

That was too much. Lydia found herself shaking with anger.

"She did, did she? You and Mrs. Bates seem to have had a good talk."

Lydia sipped her coffee and gave in to her anger. Really! Agatha Bates had no business whatsoever talking about Lydia's personal life and speculating that Ralph might have been murdered. What did she think she was doing?

10

Dressed and having her third and last cup of coffee, Lydia Prescott discovered she was still angry. That wasn't like her. What was Agatha Bates up to? Lydia decided she would call her Monday morning when the girls were at school and remind Agatha that *she* was their mother and knew what was best for them.

She didn't have to wait until Monday. She was rolling up the bills Kate had separated to put in the coffee can under the counter when she heard a knock at the door.

"I'll get it," Kate shouted, and raced to the door. "It's Agatha," she called. "Hi, Agatha."

"May I come in, Kate?"

"Sure. Mom's still having breakfast. It's her day off."

"That's good," Lydia heard Agatha say. "She's the one I want to talk to."

Lydia felt mollified. Agatha had come to apologize. She swung around on her stool toward the door. "I'm afraid there's no more coffee," she said. "The little pot only holds three cups."

"That's all right, Lydia. I've had my one cup of instant. That's all I allow myself these days. I'm sorry to bother you on your day off. I tried to call this morning, but the operator wouldn't give me your number. She said it was unlisted. So I decided to come by in person."

Sandy was listening to Agatha. "That's because Dad didn't want it listed. He said we lived in a pretty lonely part of town and some people liked to play games on the telephone."

"You didn't tell me that, Sandy," Lydia said. "You just told me your father said it was better to have an unlisted number. You didn't tell me why." But Sandy had told Agatha right off. Lydia would have to get that relationship straight once and for all.

"I'm sorry, Mom," Sandy apologized. She had made a mistake. She went back to Kate's room to watch the noon movie.

"I've hurt her feelings," Lydia said. "They're very sensitive about their father. That's what I wanted to talk to you about, Agatha. . . ."

Before she could get started, Agatha unfolded two flannel-wrapped packages she had taken from her jacket pocket. She placed two objects on the counter. "I came about these," she announced.

"What are they?" Lydia asked in surprise.

"They are ivory carvings, probably walrus ivory. One is a bear, the other is a knife. I'm pretty certain they are very old. If they are, they must be extremely valuable."

"And so?" Lydia said, almost rudely. She was exasperated. What was Agatha up to now, showing her two old pieces of ivory?

"They belong to Sandy and Kate, unless they belong to

someone else first," Agatha explained. "The girls weren't interested in them and agreed I should keep them to find out what they are."

"Where did my girls get something like these?"

"From your husband. They were wrapped up in birthday paper at the bottom of one of his clothes cartons."

"I don't know anything about that," Lydia said. "I didn't pay much attention to that stuff. I'm going to give it to the Salvation Army. You can give them these things, too. We don't want any of Ralph's junk around here. The girls were right. They don't need stuff like that."

Lydia was going to be more difficult than Agatha had anticipated. "You aren't interested in how old these artifacts are?"

"No."

"Nor how your husband came to have them?"

That was too much! First, Ralph may have been murdered. Now he was a thief. "Are you implying Ralph stole them, Mrs. Bates? I don't want any of that talk around Sandy and Kate. You've told them enough already; too much, in fact. I'm not ashamed of being a waitress, but I'd like to tell Sandy and Kate about my life myself." Lydia's voice rose. She brought it under control. "And please don't suggest to them that Ralph might have been mixed up in something crooked. He may have been an alcoholic, Mrs. Bates, and done things to us he shouldn't have done, but I can tell you that he was as honest as the day is long. Ralph would never have stolen a penny from anyone." She began to sob and put her hands over her face.

"Please, Lydia. I'm very sorry. I realized as soon as I pointed out the café we were passing to Sandy and Kate that it was none of my business. But they were so excited to learn something about *you,* as well as about their father, I had to tell them it was where you and Ralph met. It was important to them."

Agatha paused. Lydia had turned away from her. "And so are these artifacts. And so is three hundred thousand dollars. And so is the rest of your life and your children's lives." Agatha didn't want to say the insurance would get them out of a mobile home in a lonely pine grove. "I'm sorry to be so blunt," she apologized. "I'm a widow, too. We can't live in the past, whether it was good or bad. You want to forget it and I want to remember it, but in the meantime we have to live in the present."

Lydia shook her head. "I can't help you. I don't know what Ralph was up to and I don't want to and I don't want my children to know."

"Please come with me, Lydia. That's all I'm asking. It's important. There's a woman who lives on the town forest road named Mavis Langhorne. Chief Torbert says she is as eccentric as I am. I want to show these to her."

"What for?" Lydia asked. "To find out if they are stolen?"

"I doubt she will know that. No, to find out whether they are genuine and where they came from. I don't think your husband stole them, either, Lydia, if that's any consolation. They were given to Sandy and Kate by their father. He wouldn't give them stolen goods as a birthday present, would he?"

"I'm not sure now. The Ralph I knew never would have had things like these in his possession. All he knew or cared about was cars, used and new."

Agatha wrapped up the ivory objects. She stuffed them carefully back into her pocket. "Let's go see Dr. Langhorne. We can talk about the rest of it on the way. Will Sandy and Kate be all right by themselves?"

"They've spent the last three years by themselves. I'll get my coat."

"I was the juvenile officer for several years," Agatha said, as they drove through the center of town. "Life can be very cruel to children—not life really, but their parents, neighbors, grown-ups, their friends, and even the police. It wasn't my job to help them, only to keep track of them. I learned two things: one, that their lives were sometimes hard beyond belief, and two, they all needed to talk about themselves."

"Are you telling me I have to keep going back over our years with Ralph in Henderson? I won't do that."

"No, that's not the point, Lydia. You have to talk with them about what's going on now and answer their questions honestly. Kate is half traumatized by the circumstances of your husband's death. You know that better than I do. Sandy is upset and tries not to show it so as not to trouble her mother. You know that, too. That is why you're angry with me. Let the good part of your marriage come out. They already know the bad part."

Lydia did not respond at once. Then she said, "What about what's going on now? Are you trying to prove Ralph may have been murdered? That's absurd. Officer Trudeau would have told me if they thought that. Do you want to drag them into a murder case? I won't have it. I simply won't have it."

"Officer Trudeau saw the old Ralph and what he saw made sense to him. The girls heard another Ralph on the phone, maybe the one you used to listen to in the City Line Café, the one you fell in love with and married. Try to

61

understand that the girls and I think that's the Ralph Prescott who died. He didn't jump off the bridge. He didn't throw himself down a muddy riverbank. He may have slipped. I honestly don't know. But I can tell you, we're not talking about the Ralph Prescott you left three years ago."

"Is that all?" Lydia asked.

"Not quite. I think he was scared of something or someone."

"What do you want from me, Agatha? I can't tell you anything that matters. I only remember the man you call the old Ralph."

"What I want from you is for you to tell me it's all right if I talk to Trudeau again, if I talk to Don Ostel in the mill, if I talk to some car rental agencies, if I talk to the people in the Henderson post office. Most of all, I want you to tell me it's all right if I talk to Kate and Sandy about what I am doing and ask them about their talks on the phone with Ralph. He's bound to have said something about himself that they didn't pay any attention to. There mustn't be mysteries any longer for them. Maybe they'd like to come along with me sometimes. They'll find out some things about the Ralph Prescott none of us knew."

"You want my girls taking part in a murder investigation?" Lydia asked in horror.

"No. I want them to find out the truth about their father. Something tells me it's not a bad truth, Lydia. I can't forget those three boxes of freshly laundered, neatly packed clothes. He was proud of himself. We can't bring him back, but we can find a father for them to remember."

They were approaching the town forest road. Agatha pulled over to the side. She turned in her seat to face Lydia

Prescott. "We are talking about their future, Lydia. There's nothing wrong with money, I can tell you. The insurance people aren't going to pay out unless they have to. If Ralph wanted you to have it, you should have it."

Lydia turned her eyes away from Agatha to stare into the dark hemlocks along the road. Agatha Bates was a hard woman. "You will see that they aren't hurt?" she asked at last.

"That I promise. I can't stop once I begin, because if my suspicions are right, I must go on, and so will the police, but I will protect them from things they shouldn't know. That I promise."

Lydia nodded assent. "It will be all right if they tell me what's going on? They had secrets with Ralph over the phone, because they didn't want to upset me. But not telling me hurt even more."

"No secrets, Lydia. I promise that, too. No secrets."

Two enormous black dogs lumbered up to the car, barking
loudly and wagging their bushy tails at the same time to show
they didn't mean it. Lydia bent down to scratch one under the
chin. "We had a big black-and-white mutt back home," she
told Agatha. "All he did was lie on the kitchen floor waiting
for a handout. Do you think the girls should have a dog?"

Agatha detected anxiety in her question. Lydia's relationship with Sandy and Kate had been shaken. Her husband's calls to the girls, the insurance, and his sudden
death brought problems she had trouble facing. She had
been frank with Lydia this far, Agatha thought; she might
as well continue.

"I think it might be a good idea, if both you and the girls
understand you are not trying to buy their affection. The
dog should belong to all three of you. Don't let what has
happened split you off from the girls. Let's ask Dr. Langhorne about dogs. Our family never had one."

The door to the shack opened and a short, square
woman in corduroy trousers and an old army jacket came

toward them, calling to her dogs to shut up. Agatha was surprised to see that Dr. Langhorne was, like her, in her sixties. For no reason whatsoever, she had expected to meet a younger woman.

"Dr. Langhorne?" she said.

"That's right. You mustn't mind these monsters. They have nothing better to do all day out here in the woods than bark at whatever passes. The Carters"—She nodded toward a big white house a hundred yards down the road.—"aren't speaking to me anymore. They say Jack and Mary Ann keep them awake at night. Silly people. Dogs are supposed to bark."

"Chief Torbert suggested we come see you. This is Lydia Prescott, who is going to ask you about a dog for her girls later, I hope, and I am Agatha Bates. We have really come about another matter."

"Torbert sent you, did he? Did he say I was the town crazy?"

"In a way," Agatha admitted. "He put you in the same category with me—meddling women, I suppose."

"Oh, Malcolm's all right. The Carters got after him about Jack and Mary Ann, and he felt that he had to come out and fuss at me for appearance' sake. He said Carter can't stand his wife, so he takes it out on the dogs. Carter also thinks my shack keeps the value of his property down. Come on in."

It was not a shack inside, Lydia noted. It was bright, attractive, and, most of all, comfortable. It was much larger than her mobile home.

"Is the kitchen all right?" Dr. Langhorne asked. "It's the only place where I have three chairs. The sofa is full of dog hairs. It's where they sleep in the winter."

65

"This table is better," Agatha said. She unwrapped the carvings again and placed them side by side in the middle of the antique pine table. "We'd be grateful if you could tell us something about these."

Mavis Langhorne studied the ivories for the longest time, it seemed to Lydia, without saying a word. She took an old-fashioned magnifying glass from the table drawer to look into the bear's throat. She hummed to herself as she worked.

At last she announced her findings. "They are Inuit— that's Eskimo—carvings from the Northwest Territories of Canada, probably the Hudson Bay area. Dorset Culture, I'd say. They aren't from my field of study, so I can't be precise. I deal with the coastal people of the eastern United States."

"Are they old?" Agatha asked.

"Oh, yes, very old. An expert could tell you just how old. I can't. More than a thousand years, I'd say. The Inuit don't work in ivory so much anymore."

"Is there any chance they are fake? I mean, could they be copies?"

Dr. Langhorne was decisive. "No, that I can tell you with absolute certainty."

"Do they have any value?" Lydia brought herself to ask.

Dr. Langhorne looked at her, Lydia thought, as though that was the stupidest question she had ever heard.

"Value? Mrs. Prescott, you can't put value on artifacts like these. They are priceless. They are museum pieces. You can buy a Rembrandt from time to time, if you have enough money. You can't buy these—at least, you shouldn't be able to. They are part of history. They are not the work of a single artist. They are the work of a people."

"What we mean," Agatha explained patiently, somewhat surprised at Dr. Langhorne's outburst, "is not the cash value of the carvings, but their value as what they are."

"I can only repeat that they are priceless, if it is any help to you. Would it be too much to ask where they came from? An old trunk in the attic, something like that?"

"They are birthday presents to my daughters," Lydia said proudly. "Their father gave them to Sandy and Kate just before he died. We don't know where he acquired them."

"Well, I suppose crazier things have happened in my business. There is a famous stone in my museum down in Boston. An Indian found it near a seaport in Central America. It had carvings on it. By good luck it ended up in the hands of an archeologist. The carvings turned out to be a kind of translation of some words from one language we didn't know into one we did know. It helped us understand the principal Indian culture of the whole region. A priest must have made the carving a thousand years ago for some reason. That is what I mean by priceless, Mrs. Prescott. I'd bet my life that these are the only two Inuit carvings of their kind in existence. Others from the same area, yes. Others from the same period, yes. But these are one of a kind, like almost all the carvings from that time. You have no idea where Mr. Prescott obtained them?"

"None," Lydia replied.

"Do you know if anyone in his background was an Arctic explorer?"

The question brought a bitter smile to Lydia's lips. The notion of Ralph Prescott—or even his grandfather, whom she met once—being an explorer was funny. "I don't think so," she replied. "The family were mill workers in Henderson from way back."

"I would swear they are museum pieces, but that doesn't have to mean they are. Let me see. Excuse me." Dr. Langhorne went to one of the bulging bookstands in the living room.

She brought a large book back to the table. She flipped through the pages of illustrations. "Nothing here. This is the only book I have on Inuit art. I don't see anything here that resembles your carvings. There's one person who can tell you without a shadow of a doubt what these pieces are." She turned to the title page and pointed to a name. "Professor Gaston Le Maître. He is the world's foremost authority on Inuit culture."

"I'm not sure that does us much good right now. He is a Canadian, is he not?"

"Yes." Dr. Langhorne looked at the inside of the book jacket. "He's not so far away, if he's still alive. He's at Laval University in Quebec. That's not more than two hundred and fifty miles from here. Why, I even hiked up there one summer."

"Well, I guess that's it for now," Agatha said. "Thank you. You have been very helpful."

"The dog, Agatha," Lydia whispered. "Do we have time to talk about a dog for the girls?"

"I'm sorry, Lydia. I forgot all about it. I have all the time in the world."

"Do you like dogs, Mrs. Prescott?" Dr. Langhorne asked. She suddenly seemed friendlier. "You know, I never had anything to do with them until I got Jack and Mary Ann. They have changed my life entirely. Now I have two friends and no neighbors. Used to be I had neighbors and no friends. What about dogs, Mrs. Prescott?"

Lydia said she lived on the other side of town, off Old

Winthrop Road. "Five days a week, I'm at work from mid-morning until late at night in Winthrop. I have two girls. They need company and someone to look after. I think I'd like a dog again, too," she added shyly.

"You're right. We all need a dog. The bigger the better, I say. I wouldn't trade my two Newfies for a hundred of these." She pointed to the ivory carvings.

"Not too big, perhaps. We live in a small house."

"Big house, little house, they will always be in your way," Dr. Langhorne said cheerfully. "A good dog sticks close to the family. You'll get used to it. I don't suppose you want to pay a lot of money for one. You shouldn't have to pay for a dog, anyway."

"I'm afraid I can't, Dr. Langhorne," Lydia said.

"Mavis. Call me Mavis. I stopped being a doctor the day I quit the museum. That was the smartest thing I ever did. It gave me time to become the town eccentric. Right, Agatha?"

Agatha didn't answer. What a strange woman, she thought. No, that was wrong, not strange at all. Mavis Langhorne was being herself, probably for the first time in her life.

"Look, Lydia, I'll walk over to see my cousin Esther tomorrow. She lives in Upton. She breeds Newfoundlands. She gave me Jack and Mary Ann. They weren't show dogs and she didn't want to sell them, so I got them. How about that? The last time I was over there, she had a male with one blue and one brown eye. She didn't want to sell him, either. He must be six months old now, if she hasn't given him away."

"How big would he be?" Lydia asked fearfully.

"Pretty big, but not as big as these clowns yet. They're

very gentle dogs, Lydia. Great with kids. But they do make a lot of noise when someone comes by. Do you have neighbors?"

Lydia shook her head. She turned to Agatha as if to accuse her of getting her into a situation she didn't want to be in. "What do you think, Agatha? They seem awfully big to me."

"It's for you to decide, Lydia, if the dog is available. Wouldn't you feel better if the girls had a big dog at the house? You said you were worried about them. Ralph was too, apparently."

Mavis jumped up from the table. "I'll go down to the Carters' and borrow their phone. I'll call Esther to see if Two Eyes is still there. Come on, you two." She prodded the two monsters under the table. "It's time for a walk."

Agatha was amused. She couldn't help asking Mavis if the Carters, who weren't speaking to her, minded sharing their phone with her.

"Oh, they're always glad to see me," Mavis replied. "They're lonely people. Anyway, it gives them a chance to complain about Jack and Mary Ann. They like to complain."

12

Agatha found a folded note slipped under the door: "I've talked with Webb, the insurance man. Come over for tea or supper when you get back. Arthur."

Maybe Lydia can collect enough insurance money to pay for a dog, Agatha thought wryly. The trip to Mavis Langhorne's had not been as productive as she'd hoped. Mavis had chiefly confirmed her suspicions about the carvings; Agatha felt good about that. As for a trip to Quebec City, it would have to come after she found out some other things.

And there was the dog, or the possible dog. For reasons she wasn't able to explain to herself, Agatha had promised Lydia she would take the half-grown puppy if Mavis found him still available and he didn't work out at the Prescott house.

It would work out, she assured herself. A puppy was the very thing to distract Kate from her morbid fantasies about her father. If worse came to worst, her Tom would have to live with the odd-eyed Newfoundland. It would probably do Tom good.

Agatha looked at her watch. It was close to five. She might as well eat supper with the Harpers. Alice was a fine cook. Even her leftovers were tastier than anything Agatha was able to put together.

"Come in, Agatha," Arthur greeted her. "Sit by the fire and have some sherry. I'm burning one of your dead branches, as a matter of fact."

Agatha sniffed. Something good was going on in the kitchen. "What's Alice making?" she asked.

"Alice is roasting a chicken," Arthur's wife said as she came into the living room. "A big one. It will more than feed the three of us nicely and take care of Arthur for the rest of the week. I'm having a vacation from the kitchen."

"What did Mr. Webb say?" Agatha asked.

"Just about what I expected him to say. The police in Henderson have listed Prescott's death as a probable accident. Trudeau does not deny the possibility of suicide. The company disputes that it was an accident. They base their assessment on Prescott's earlier attempt on his life and the timing of his death so soon after taking on such a high-benefit policy.

"Webb sold Prescott the policy himself. Prescott wanted one for half a million. Universal wouldn't go for that. Their doctor gave him a good bill of health. When Ralph said he would put up two years' premiums in advance, they let him have a policy for three hundred thousand. Double indemnity, of course. That's standard. If Prescott had a genuine accident or, let us say, was disposed of, they have to pay six hundred thousand. A tidy sum, Agatha, a very tidy sum."

"And the suicide clause?"

"That's buried down in the policy."

"Where does that leave the Prescott children?"

"They will have to fight, I'm afraid. And it would mean dragging Ralph Prescott's character and behavior out in front of them. Their mother won't have that, you say. Oh, I almost forgot. Universal's investigator went to the bridge. He says it's pretty hard to believe someone could roll all the way down into the river, even when it was flowing higher. That's his opinion."

"No bargaining?" Agatha inquired.

"Not much. I put on my stern face and said the usual tough words. Webb assured me he was concerned about the children's grief and so on at losing their father. He said his company had a small moral responsibility for selling Prescott a policy. Not a legal responsibility, mind you. The long and short of their charity is an offer to make payment of ten thousand dollars."

"What do you think of that?"

"I think what I thought earlier: It's going to be hard to collect. Universal has the resources, and the Prescotts have none."

"Ten thousand won't get the girls very far in college these days."

"You're right. I can probably screw Webb up for another ten thousand. That will be the limit."

Now Agatha told Arthur about the carvings. "Does that change anything for you, Arthur?"

"Nothing at all. The company will argue that Prescott got tangled up in some shady business and took a way out before he was arrested. They'll say the carvings and the insurance were an attempt to look after his kids. Are you going to pursue it?"

73

"I'm going to sleep on it. I'll have a talk with Officer Trudeau. I doubt they'll reopen the case on the basis of a couple of birthday presents. We'll see. Right now, I'm going to have the first good meal I've had since the last time Alice fed me."

Agatha was waiting across the road from the school when the bell rang. First Kate, then Sandy, ran down the walk, spied the Toyota, and came running over. As they climbed in, Agatha asked Kate, "What color is it this month?"

Kate, in the front seat, looked at her blankly. "What do you mean, what color?"

"Last fall Sandy told me you chew a different color bubble gum every month. I saw your collection under the counter."

"Oh, that. Gee, I gave that up."

"Did you ever try orange? Mr. Reed at the general store said it was something new." Agatha held out two packs of gum. "One for each of you, if you want them. If you don't, give them to your friends."

As they headed toward Henderson, Agatha said, "I'm going to ask you again if you want to help me. Your mother said you could come along with me this afternoon. You may talk to whomever I talk to. We may find out a few things about your father that will surprise you, I don't know. I'm pretty sure he won't disappoint you. Frankly, you wouldn't be going with me if I thought that. I doubt that I would be here myself."

"The insurance company thinks he jumped off the bridge, don't they?" Kate asked.

"That's certainly what they want to think."

"What do *you* really think, Agatha?" Sandy asked.

74

"That's what I am trying to find out. If I hadn't seen his apartment and the carvings, I'd probably think he slipped, maybe that he slipped on purpose."

"He left the presents in the box for us," Kate said. "Why did he wrap them up so long before our birthdays?"

"That's a good point, Kate. I don't know."

"Mom says some woman over in the town forest says the little carvings are priceless. Is that so?" Sandy asked.

"Yes. I doubt they will ever belong to you, frankly. Sooner or later we may make a trip up to Quebec City to show them to an expert. He'll know where they came from."

"Dad stole them, then?"

"Of course not. Do you think your father would have given you something stolen for your birthday? No, I'm certain that's not what happened. Listen to me, please, both of you. I want you to remember as much as you can of what your father said to you the times he called you up. If you remember something, write it down so you won't forget, even if it seems unimportant. You may hear or see things that will make you remember. Business things, for example. What was he doing? Did he travel? Why didn't he call you up for four or five days every once in a while? Where did he call you from? There was no phone in his place. Did he say why you couldn't call him? Your father is a mystery man to me."

"Why all the trouble?" Sandy was curious. Agatha seemed very determined about Dad. "Is it the insurance? We don't care about that. We don't really think he jumped, do we, Kate? Mom says the police are right. Dad may have been drunk and slipped. When we had a place on the third floor in Henderson, he had a lot of trouble with the steps."

They were coming into Henderson, and Agatha began looking for the signs Trudeau had given her to the police station. "Is that how you want to remember your father, Sandy, falling down the steps because he couldn't stand up?"

Sandy shrugged. "I guess not."

"You were pretty pleased with him when you were talking to him, weren't you?"

"Yes."

"Well, let's see if we can find that father for you, even if it means something not very good happened to him."

13

Officers Trudeau and Melankamp met with Agatha Bates and the Prescott girls around a rickety table in a noisy little room. Agatha explained that the three of them were uncertain about what might have happened to Ralph Prescott the rainy night he died. They had no intention of questioning Sergeant Trudeau's report, but it seemed that the insurance company had made it clear *they* did not accept the findings for an accidental death.

Trudeau was silent. He let Melankamp answer. "I can understand your confusion," Melankamp said smoothly. "I can also understand what the insurance people want to believe. Look, our experience tells us it was probably an accident, and that is how Paul here put it down after his investigation: 'probable cause of death, accidental drowning.' We have no evidence to the contrary.

"I remember your involvement with running down the man who was holding Kate here last fall, Lieutenant Bates. Chief Torbert tells me you were with the Boston police for a number of years. When there was an accident, and you had no evidence or suspicion to think otherwise, you accepted the obvious, right?" Melankamp paused before he continued, looking across the table at Sandy and Kate, who were sitting straight up in metal folding chairs, listening intently. "Your father had a drinking problem, I guess," he began.

"We know about that," Sandy said. "It's all we can remember about him, his drinking, isn't it, Kate?"

Kate nodded. "We went away with our mother because we couldn't live with him anymore," Kate said. "But that doesn't mean we didn't love him. We did. And we still do."

"Kate," Trudeau spoke for the first time. "I am the officer who looked into what happened to your father. I explained it all to your mother. There was nothing else I could tell her. Some other police officers saw him on the bridge that night. They knew who your father was and they waved to him. He waved back. Your father was a friendly man most of the time. But he did have his problems. Do you understand?"

Trudeau leaned toward Kate and Sandy. Very gently he told them that Ralph Prescott had been found the next morning between some rocks out in the river. "We went to where he used to live, an old boardinghouse across the river from the mill. We sometimes helped him to find his way home. We didn't know he had moved, you see."

That was news to Agatha. "You went there first?" she inquired.

"We did, Lieutenant Bates. As far as we knew, it was where Ralph Prescott still lived. Mrs. Cotter told us he had given up his room six months before. He told her he was moving across the river to the old Putnam Mill. This was about a month after the accident."

"Accident?" Sandy asked. "What accident?"

"He was hit by a car, Sandy," Melankamp said. "I called the ambulance myself. He was lucky to be alive. It was a hit-and-run driver. From what a witness said, your dad walked right out in front of the car. He was pretty drunk. It turned out he was only bruised in the ribs and shoulders. They kept him at the hospital for a couple of days to be sure he was all right and turned him loose. We never found the driver."

That was interesting, Agatha thought. "So you didn't have to help him off the sidewalks after that? After he moved across the river to the mill, you used to see him on the bridge or the streets once in a while, is that correct? He didn't seem to need your help."

Melankamp and Trudeau nodded agreement.

"Why don't you tell the officers about the phone calls and the presents?" Agatha told the girls. "These seem to have begun about the time Prescott moved," she explained to the men.

By turns, the girls recounted their father's attentions. "We don't think Dad was drinking," Sandy said proudly. "He said he was going to visit us this summer."

"I think," Kate added, "I think after the car hit him he was scared of what could happen to him. He quit, that's what he did. He quit and started to be our friend."

"You're probably right," Trudeau said kindly. "But not altogether, Kate. I'm sorry to tell you that the night he fell, he had something to drink, we are certain of that."

Agatha tried to slide the discussion past the coroner's report. The girls didn't need to know about that procedure. "How much do you think, Sergeant? A can of beer? An ounce of whiskey? Something on that order?"

"More or less. It wasn't a great deal."

"But enough to make Ralph Prescott careless, perhaps? You suppose he left the bridge and was crossing over the road? Then came too close to the slope and slipped?"

"Yes, that's what I think. When we discovered where he lived, we went to the mill. The janitor showed us to his place. The door was off the latch. Afterward, I went down to the road and crossed over. It was still raining. At the corner that little path down was treacherous. They should put a fence around it. The river was running high. A week before, a teenager fell down the bank farther up the river. He held on to the rocks until we pulled him out. I really believe your father slipped that night," he said to the girls. "He went out for some fresh air and had a drink and, well, that was that."

"Fred, here," Trudeau continued, "knew about the family and where you lived. I called your mother. I had to get the phone company to give me the unlisted number. It was her day off, your mother said. She was glad she was home to answer the phone, not you girls. She came over the next day and I showed her the apartment. She didn't say much. I'm sorry, Sandy and Kate, but she did say your father might have had too much to drink and wasn't watching where he was going."

"Did Mom tell you about Dad's insurance?" Kate asked.

"She did," Trudeau said, "but not about how much. She said something to the effect that her husband was insured, at least. I found out the name of the company and got in touch with them. It was the investigator who told me the amount. We were surprised. I told him what I'm telling you. He wanted me to say I thought it was a suicide. I couldn't and I can't. Believe me, your father didn't take his own life. I will testify to that if I have to."

"And his wallet," Agatha said. "Malcolm Torbert told me Officer Melankamp said there was only a social security card and a driver's license and a few dollars. Nothing else at all?"

"Absolutely nothing. And nothing in the pockets of the suits hanging up."

"If his keys were on the table, how would he have gotten back into the mill?" Agatha asked. "It must have been closed."

"Ostel, the janitor, said the outside lock was tricky. When people went out for a short while early in the evening, they put a wedge in so they wouldn't have to fight the lock. When the night watchman came by later, he secured it for the night. It's all in my report, Lieutenant Bates. I'll have a copy made for you. I'll stand behind every word," Trudeau said defensively.

"Please don't bother. You have been very kind. I'm sure Sandy and Kate are beginning to understand." Agatha did not go into where Trudeau thought Ralph Prescott might have taken a drink. There was no sign of beer in the apartment and no bar in the vicinity of the mill. Had he gone across the bridge? That didn't seem likely to her for some reason. But it was not a matter she wanted to discuss in front of Kate and Sandy.

"What do you think about the note that went with the insurance policy?" she asked the two officers.

"Do you still have the note, Sandy?" Melankamp inquired.

Sandy shook her head.

"You are pretty sure that's what he wrote, 'If something happens to me'? You see, your mother didn't tell us about that. She really didn't want to talk about your father to Sergeant Trudeau at all."

"Not with us, either," Sandy replied. "She's upset and wants to forget about it. I guess Kate and I don't. Like Agatha says, we think we had our dad back for a while, the one we hardly ever saw."

"And these, what do you make of these?" Agatha showed Trudeau and Melankamp the two carvings.

"Carvings," Melankamp said. "What about them?"

"Dad gave them to us for our birthdays," Kate said. "He was going to, anyway, I guess. He left them for us."

"We found them at the bottom of one of the cartons of clothes. Apparently you missed them," Agatha said to Trudeau.

"I didn't touch those clothes," Trudeau said, "only the suit jackets. I left the rest for Mrs. Prescott." He picked up the bear. "These are Eskimo carvings, aren't they? Canadian, too. I was born in Canada, you know."

"Yes, I know," Agatha replied. "They are Inuit, and we have been told they are more than a thousand years old. They are priceless, Dr. Langhorne said."

"What was Ralph Prescott doing with them?" Melankamp asked. He was interested in the carvings now.

"That is what we want to know," Agatha said.

"Agatha thinks maybe Dad was pushed," Sandy said.

"I didn't say that exactly. I said it was a possibility that Officer Trudeau might want to consider."

"It doesn't figure," Trudeau said.

"It makes some sense," Agatha permitted herself to argue, "if you consider Ralph Prescott was a changed man.

Apparently he lived a sober life. Apparently he had money. He spoke to Sandy and Kate about his business. I can tell you the clothes he had were expensive. They didn't belong to an alcoholic who slept in the streets."

"Let's go take another look," Trudeau said. "Want to come along, Fred?"

"Why not?" Melankamp said.

Agatha followed the cruiser in her Toyota. Sandy had the key to Prescott's place. The door to Ostel's studio was closed, she noticed, as they went by. She unlocked the door and led the officers to the bedroom. She pointed to the clothes pole. "Over there," she said.

"Where?" asked Trudeau.

Sandy looked. The clothes on the pole were gone. The three cartons underneath were also gone.

14

"What is Officer Trudeau going to do, Agatha?" Sandy asked on the way home.

"You heard him, Sandy. He said he was going to look into it. I think he means he will talk to your friend Don Ostel. I doubt that Don has a key to your father's place. Trudeau won't find out much."

Agatha was disappointed in Trudeau's response, and Melankamp's, too. When she asked them, as a matter of courtesy, if she could look into Prescott's past, they had no objections—and no interest, either. It was clear that the case was closed as far as they were concerned. The missing clothes were another, separate case, petty larceny, which they would deal with by asking Don Ostel some questions. Agatha understood they couldn't do much more, unless they admitted there was a deeper mystery to Ralph Prescott's life and death, which they couldn't be bothered with. She could sense their impatience at having to deal with the girls and her. They had other things to do.

"Why would Don want Dad's clothes?" Kate asked. "He

already said he didn't want them. They certainly wouldn't fit him, would they?" Don Ostel was a thin, slight man. Prescott's clothes would hang on him like a scarecrow's clothes.

Without thinking, Agatha replied, "Maybe whoever took them didn't want the clothes."

"What do you mean, Agatha? What did they want?"

Agatha realized again what had been bothering her since she first entered Prescott's three rooms. It seemed like a place not to be actually lived in. She had assumed, instinctively, she supposed, that it was a workplace, a storage place, and Prescott did his living somewhere else. But Trudeau told her Prescott had moved, all of him, apparently, to the mill. The mill *was* his home.

She heard Kate again. "What did they want, then, Agatha? Do you know?"

"Tell me, Kate. You, too, Sandy. If you lived where your father lived, where would you keep your personal things? Your papers, your money, your bills, your documents, whatever important things you had? Where does your mother keep her papers?"

"In her bureau drawer," Sandy said. "She's always saying how nice it would be to have enough room for a little study with a desk and a bookshelf and a file cabinet to put junk in."

"Exactly. Where was your father's bureau drawer? You both looked around for things that belonged to him. What did you find?"

"Nothing. A razor and some soap in the bathroom, and a towel. Nothing in the refrigerator. An empty soup can and some eggshells in the trash bag. A couple of plates and a cup and a glass and two pans next to the hot plate. And some silverware in one of those boxes, like the ones on the table."

"If you lived there, where would you put your personal things?"

"With my clothes," Kate piped up from the backseat. "I keep my valentines and money and pictures and my jewelry in my sock drawer."

"Did you find anything in your dad's clothes boxes?" Agatha asked.

"We only looked in one," Sandy explained. "We found the birthday presents and didn't go into the other two."

"That's what I thought," Agatha said. "Isn't it possible that someone walked off with the cartons and the hanging clothes because he—or she—was looking for something?"

"Like what?" Kate wanted to know.

"Like something that wasn't there," Agatha said. "Like something you found all wrapped up in birthday paper with your names outside."

"The carvings! Someone wanted them," Sandy almost shouted. "You said they were priceless. They are worth a lot of money, aren't they?" She paused. "The same guy might have pushed Dad, just the way you thought. Is that what you think, Agatha?"

"More or less," Agatha responded. "I think someone had a key or took your father's keys and went to the apartment that night and tried to find the carvings. He was probably in a hurry and didn't pay any attention to two birthday packages. Later, he decided to go back and have another look. Maybe he remembered the birthday boxes. He came back this weekend and cleaned out everything. He must have been in a hurry again."

"He's going to be disappointed," Sandy said.

"That's right, Sandy. He is. What we have to do is find out all we can about your father. That should take us pretty close to that person. Sergeant Trudeau won't do much unless we lead him along."

"Will we be coming back to Henderson some afternoons?" Kate asked.

"If you want to come," Agatha said. "I may have to look in a couple of places by myself while you are in school. We don't have much time after school."

"That's great," Kate said. "I won't have to do my homework every afternoon."

"No, but you will have to do it every night. That is part of our agreement."

As the Toyota pulled up the dirt driveway to the girls' house, the outside light over the steps clicked on. Lydia stood behind the glass panels of the storm door, watching Agatha and the girls climb out of the car. Then she pushed the door open. An awkward black beast hurtled down the steps toward the car. He danced around Sandy and Kate, charging toward them and dashing away when they tried to touch him. He sniffed at the Toyota's tires and ran down the driveway. He stopped, inviting them to chase him.

Lydia came up to her daughters. She hugged the speechless Kate. When Kate squeezed loose to chase the puppy, Lydia put her arm around Sandy.

"Dr. Langhorne and her cousin came by this afternoon. They left that crazy puppy. He's had all his shots for a year. She even left a big bag of food and his feeding dish and a leash. He's going to need a new collar in a month or so."

The Newfoundland let Kate trap him. Breathless, he lay across her lap, panting and wagging his tail. Sandy knelt beside them. She scratched the silky head and ears. "What's his name?" she called to her mother.

"Esther said he didn't have a name yet. She's been calling him Newfy. She said he'll get used to whatever you decide."

"What do you want to call him, Kate?" Sandy asked.

"Gee, I don't know. I haven't had time to think about it. Are Prince or Duke good names? They're not fancy, but he might like them. Which do you prefer, Sandy?"

"Let's call him Duke. That sounds better."

"Okay," Kate said. "Let's go inside and see what there is to eat."

Sandy and Kate went into the house, Duke following at their heels.

"He looks like a nice dog, Lydia."

"Oh, he is. I feel like a mother again." She laughed. "He'll work out. We won't have to ask you to look after him."

Thank the Lord for small favors, Agatha thought. One yellow tomcat was quite enough for her simple life.

15

I am not a detective, Agatha Bates thought. In fact, I never was a real detective. It was just a title they gave me. She couldn't remember a genuine mystery case in her whole career. Now, at the end of it, she was only a retired police officer who somehow had been drawn into the death of an ex-drunk who just happened to be the father of two girls she was very fond of.

It was ridiculous, no matter how you looked at it. Henderson was a small city thirty miles away that she had visited only two or three times before the recent events. It was a maze of streets she couldn't locate, some of which didn't go anywhere after she did find them. She had no authority to back her, only a kind of unofficial permission from the police department to ask questions about a man they said died of an accident.

Ultimately, she supposed, Paul Trudeau might take an interest, but for the moment both he and Fred Melankamp had made it clear they didn't want to be involved. In fact, she was alone on a case for the first time ever. Not altogether alone, of course. She had two partners, the twelve-year-old Sandy Prescott and her ten-year-old sister, Kate. She had their assistance for a couple of hours after school and all day Saturday. Agatha laughed softly to herself. She had had worse partners, certainly less pleasant ones, in her career.

And what exactly was she looking for? The real Ralph Prescott, she told Lydia and the girls, a new and different husband and father who would change the unhappy memories his family had of the old Ralph Prescott. There was always the chance, she realized, that the new Ralph might be worse than the old one.

There was the insurance money, to be sure. If it became available, there was no question that it would provide a better future for the Prescotts. Beyond that, she had to admit, was the mystery. Something was wrong. Bits and pieces of information didn't fit. There were things missing between the pieces. The big question was Ralph Prescott himself. What new identity had he assumed after an accident that put him briefly in a hospital?

That seemed the place to start—without the girls. They could stay home for a day with their puppy.

First, she had to talk to Arthur Harper and Malcolm Torbert. Agatha felt the need for conversation and moral support.

She rang Arthur. "What happens if you don't follow up right away in the Prescott case?" she asked.

"Nothing, for a while. Eventually the company will have to get it off their books."

"Sooner or later, Lydia will probably want to settle. It's natural enough. She will tell herself it was like she won the lottery. Well, let's leave it alone for a while, Arthur. Could you tell Webb, if he gets in touch, that Lydia is undecided on what to do?"

"Sure, I'll do that. What are you up to, Agatha?"

"Honestly, Arthur, I don't know. Whatever it is, I don't want an insurance investigator poking around in it at the same time. I'm probably getting ready to make a fool of myself. Deep down, what bothers me is that there is a mystery here, and no one cares very much, except two kids. For their sake, I'd like to get it straight."

"You don't like the police report; is that it?"

"I haven't even seen it, but you're right, I don't like it. It starts with a wrong assumption. I'll talk with Torbert. He may have something to say."

Torbert didn't have much to say. He listened attentively to Agatha's speculations and shrugged.

"What you are saying, Agatha, is that Ralph Prescott didn't slip. You say he was pushed because you found some rare carvings in a box of clothes and because, afterward, the clothes disappeared. It's not Trudeau's business to worry about old Eskimo carvings. And you are right to assume he won't make much of an effort to find the clothes. Look, they disappeared three weeks after the man's death. What would he be trying to prove? He has made his report. Ask yourself what else he could put down. Probable suicide? Probably homicide? He's going by the book, Agatha. You know that."

Agatha did know that. She changed the subject. "What about your friend Melankamp?"

"He's not my friend. I never met him. We talked, both times Kate ran off, about where her father was or what he was up to. Yesterday we talked about ex-Lieutenant Agatha Bates."

"What do you mean, Malcolm?"

"Oh, he checked in here after you left. He just wanted to be sure you weren't going to cause them any trouble. He says you can talk to anyone you want to, but you mustn't represent yourself as a police officer—or a private detective, unless you have a license."

"What did you say, Malcolm, that I was a meddling old woman who wouldn't listen to you?"

"No." Torbert was serious. "I said you were a deputy officer in the town of Wingate, which didn't give you any special clout in Henderson, but I would still appreciate some professional courtesy from them. You have your badge. Go on and use it if it will help. I'll back you up."

Agatha was touched. "Thanks, Malcolm. I appreciate it."

"I don't know what happened to Prescott any more than you do," Torbert said, "but I know the Prescott kids and their mother. It's about time something good came their way. Half a million in insurance would help. Good luck, Agatha. I'm always here, except on the Fourth of July, when I'm directing traffic in front of the general store. Take care of yourself."

There was no point in bothering Melankamp to find out which hospital Prescott had been taken to. The Yellow Pages told her there were two hospitals in Henderson, the city hospital and St. Agnes.

Helen Murphy in the records office of St. Agnes was friendly. She asked only that Agatha identify herself. She brought a folder to the counter. Ralph Prescott, 17 River Street, Henderson. Received in emergency room September 17. Discharged September 19. Treated for bruises. Examined for possible internal injuries. X rays negative.

"And the bill?" Agatha said.

Mrs. Murphy rustled through the papers. "It was a little over eighteen hundred dollars. It was paid in full before his discharge."

That *was* interesting. Where did Ralph Prescott lay his hands on such a big sum? "Paid by check or credit card, can you tell me?" Agatha asked.

"It was paid in cash, apparently. That's the notation here. Highly unusual, I must say. Our records do not indicate that Mr. Prescott was well off."

"Do they tell you he was a chronic drinker?"

"I cannot answer that question, Mrs. Bates."

"Would the cashier remember the payment, do you think?"

"I'll see, just a minute." Mrs. Murphy returned with an efficient-looking young woman. "This is Miss Hubbard."

Miss Hubbard studied the statement. "This is Nancy's writing," she said. "I remember her telling me. Someone paid for Mr. Prescott. Nancy said he gave her two one-thousand-dollar bills. She said she almost dropped her teeth. The man apologized. It was all he had. He assured her they weren't counterfeit. That's all we talked about in the office for a couple of days. I had never seen a thousand-dollar bill. I still haven't."

"Neither have I, Miss Hubbard. Could I talk to Nancy?"

"I'm afraid not. She took off to California, where she came from, the day after the first snowstorm this past winter. She wasn't going to go through another one of our winters, she said."

"Would any of the nurses remember Ralph Prescott?" Agatha asked.

93

"You could go to the third floor, east wing. That's the ward he was in. I suppose it's all right."

Nurse Drago remembered Prescott without any difficulty. The patient was an alcoholic. He was in awful condition when they brought him up from emergency. Not from the accident, she told Agatha, but from drink. He was filthy, unshaven, his clothes in tatters. "They shouldn't have turned him loose," Nurse Drago said. "But they had no reason to hold him. I often wonder what happened to him."

"He drowned three weeks ago," Agatha told her.

"That figures. He was a nice guy, but you could see he wasn't long for this world."

"It's odd, don't you think, that he could pay his bill?" Agatha suggested.

"*He* didn't pay it," Nurse Drago said. "It was the visitor. Probably the guy who hit him, but I didn't ask."

"Prescott had a visitor?" Agatha asked in surprise.

"Just one, I think. He was supposed to have a family somewhere, but none of them showed up. The visitor must have found out Prescott was ready to be discharged. Apparently he went down to the cashier and paid. They left together. I pushed him down to the front door in a wheelchair—those are regulations—and off they went."

"What sort of man was the visitor?"

"Tall mån. Mustache and glasses, I'm pretty sure. Good-looking clothes. He made Prescott look like a scarecrow. He might have been sixty or more, but he didn't look much older than poor Ralph." The nurse paused a moment to reflect. "He had some sort of accent, not very pronounced. French Canadian, I'd say."

94

Agatha asked her last question. "You didn't hear them talk?"

"No. I seem to remember he came in quickly, said something to Prescott, went down to pay the bill, and came back to fetch him. Prescott sort of lurched when he left the wheelchair. The man took his arm. 'It's all right,' he said. 'You'll be all right from now on,' something like that."

16

Lydia was playing with Duke in front of the mobile home. Duke had a knotted towel in his teeth. He let Lydia pull one end while he held on, growling and wagging his tail furiously.

"I'm waiting for Peggy to take me to work," she told Agatha Bates. "You know, I have started to think about the girls' insurance that Ralph left. I keep thinking ten thousand dollars would more than buy us a second-hand car."

"Perhaps you should wait a bit," Agatha replied. "Arthur Harper is fairly certain he can do better than that. He'll be talking to the agent again. How's the puppy doing?"

"Oh, he's wonderful. Look at him pull on the towel. He's as strong as an ox. He slept in Kate's room last night, which made her feel pretty special. Sandy is a little bit jealous. And he's housebroken, too, aren't you, Duke?" She let go of the towel. "I was thinking," she confided, "that I could pay Esther for him and get rid of a few other bills hanging over us. It makes me feel uneasy to be in debt."

"Wait a few days, Lydia. The company might become afraid you will take them to court. They'll up their offer. What I came about is to ask you whether your husband spoke French or had any French Canadian friends."

"French, hah!" Lydia snorted. "Ralph didn't learn anything in school, he used to say, except how to run with a football and smile at the girls. He never mentioned any friends I can remember. He said I was the first real friend he ever had."

"Somebody paid his bill at the hospital. Did the girls tell you Ralph was hit by a car?"

"They did, and about the missing box of clothes, too. I think I'll give everything that's left to Ostel. He seemed to be as poor as we are. I don't know what you're trying to find out, Agatha, but please don't do it for my sake. I've learned to do without Ralph Prescott. If the guy that hit him paid the bill at Saint Agnes, that's fine with me. If he hadn't, the hospital might have tried to collect from me. Ralph was still legally my husband. I guess I would have been liable."

"The nurse was pretty frank about his condition," Agatha said. "It was a good thing Sandy and Kate weren't there to hear. We're going to see Ostel this afternoon. I'll bring them here to let the puppy out first. I'll tell Ostel to take what's left, if that's what you want."

"Please don't think I'm not grateful for what you are doing with Sandy and Kate. Kate has already begun to come around in little ways. The kidnapping and her father's death were almost too much for her."

"It's a pleasure for me. I almost never see my own kids and grandchildren. My life is lonely. Anyway, I'll feed them supper and get them back here in time to do their homework. Tomorrow we'll go to the post office and maybe to the old boardinghouse Ralph lived in."

The discount stores on the first floor of the Putnam Mill were having Spring Sale Days. The parking lot was filled. The spring sale seemed to be a big event in Henderson. People even wandered up to the second floor, Ostel explained, and bought artwork.

"I haven't sold anything yet," he told Agatha and Sandy and Kate. "I put a couple of my paintings outside against the wall. I think they scared people away. What can I do for you? Trudeau said you might come by. He came to ask about your father's clothes. Some of the boxes disappeared, he said."

"We found some old carvings in one of the boxes," Sandy explained. "We didn't look in the others. When we came back, they had disappeared. We thought maybe he had his papers in one of them."

"Trudeau didn't say what was missing. He wanted to know how someone got into the apartment. I couldn't help him. I don't have a key to the new lock. It wasn't broken into. Someone had a key or picked the lock."

"Lydia Prescott said you could have whatever was left," Agatha said. "Keep it or give it away, as you choose."

"I told her I'd take the little refrigerator and the hot plate. Some of my friends along the hall could use the other stuff. I'm sorry about the clothes. Ralph was pretty pleased with them. You could tell from the way he wore them. Once a week he went to the Laundromat. He brought his clothes back neatly folded in one of the boxes."

"My father was poor for a long time," Kate told him. "He didn't have a regular job until he went into business."

"I gather he had problems. I never asked. He told me a couple of times he had a new lease on life. He was proud of himself."

"How did he dress?" Agatha asked. "There were a couple of suits and a jacket and pants hanging up in the apartment. They're gone, too. Did you ever see him in a suit?"

"A few times. I'm not always here. I teach art part time at the Catholic school. When I'm really working, I close my door. That reminds me." Don Ostel rooted around in the corner of his studio. He unrolled a large piece of drawing paper. "I did this one day when Ralph stopped by. He was standing over there in a suit, looking out the window. The light was just right. I asked him not to move and made this sketch."

A tall man was standing sideways, his face half turned to the window. Agatha was astonished. "Why, he looks like a banker or an executive," she said to Sandy and Kate, who were trying to detect some resemblance in the sketch to the father they remembered.

"That's what I thought," Ostel said. "I hadn't seen Ralph dressed like that before. He was pleased with himself. I decided to do a quick sketch. 'When I'm rich,' he said, 'I'll sit for a real portrait.' Here, Sandy and Kate, you girls take it."

"Why was he dressed up?" Sandy asked.

"I don't remember what he said. He might have been going off somewhere."

"Did he talk about us?" Kate wanted to know.

"Sometimes. He said he had two girls who lived not far away and he hadn't seen them for a while."

"Did he ever have a phone in his apartment?" Agatha asked.

"No. There's a pay phone on the first floor. He used that, I know. Once he borrowed mine for a local call. It sounded like he was renting a car, maybe a van. I saw him with a van a few times."

"An ordinary van?" Agatha asked.

"Yeah, you know, the kind with a sliding door on the side. A delivery van."

"For the cartons?"

"Right. I don't know what he needed a van for, though. A while back, in January, maybe, he was unloading outside. It was icy underfoot. I offered to help. Ralph said he could manage. There were only a few boxes. He carried them up himself."

"They were sealed?" Agatha asked.

"I don't know. The tops were closed. They didn't seem very heavy."

"Was this a regular delivery?" Agatha persisted.

"I can't say, Mrs. Bates. Two or three times with the van. And sometimes with a car. I didn't pay much attention. It's pretty busy downstairs. Someone is usually loading or unloading."

"The last time we were here," Agatha reminded Ostel, "you said Ralph Prescott carried out smaller boxes once in a while."

"I did. I think he was going to the post office. There's a branch office a couple of blocks down the street. He used to put them in the trunk of the car, too. Now that I think about it, they were the days he wore a suit."

Agatha pondered what Ostel had told them. "What do you make of this, Sandy?" she asked. "Your father said he was in business. And there were periods of days when he didn't call you two up."

Sandy pondered the question. "It looks like he brought some things in and unloaded them and carried things out. I guess he was a salesman. That's what they seem to do in this old mill, sell things."

Agatha hadn't thought of that. Of course, that's why Prescott was in this building. "You're right, Sandy. I think your father was a jobber like some of the people downstairs. But I doubt that he was dealing in sweaters and shoes.

"Tell me," she said to Ostel, "did Ralph have any friends or customers who came up to his place?"

Ostel shook his head. "I can't say for sure, but I don't think so. I'm the only one he talked to, probably because I'm here a lot."

"What did he say to you?" Kate asked.

"He usually listened," Ostel replied. "I suppose I did most of the talking. I get pretty lonely here. Your father didn't talk much about himself."

"Like with us on the phone," Kate said. "He always asked what *we* were up to."

"It's like I told Trudeau," Ostel said. "It wasn't that he had any secret he was holding back on. He was just a quiet man, sort of private with himself. Like when he was staring out the window. What was he thinking then? All I know is that he went away and he came back. He never said where he went, and I didn't ask."

"We have a pretty good idea of where he went," Agatha said. "It won't be hard to find out. Let's go, Sandy and Kate. We'll have pizza in the mall. We'll come back to see Don another day. He's been very helpful."

101

17

"Let's see if I have it straight again," Kate said. "We go in and ask if there's any mail for Ralph Prescott and—"

Sandy interrupted. "Kate, we've been over this a hundred times. I know what we're going to say."

"Yeah, Sandy. I know you know. So do I. I just want to be sure, if you don't mind. We ask for Dad's mail and if the man says who? or something, we say Ralph Prescott, our dad, who brought in the packages to be mailed."

"And if they ask for a box number," Sandy added, "we look sort of dumb and say we don't know anything about a box number."

"Perfect," Agatha said. "Your father almost certainly used this branch office. He wasn't going to carry his boxes to the main office."

Things didn't work quite the way Agatha prepared them to expect, Sandy explained, when they came back to the Toyota. She and Kate had marched straight into the post office, which was a lot bigger than the one in Wingate, and

102

up to an empty counter and asked the woman for Ralph Prescott's mail.

"She wanted to know if we were his daughters right away," Kate said. "It was almost like she was expecting us. One of the people in the mill who used the post office had told her about the accident. Afterward she read about it in the paper, she said. Mom didn't tell us Dad's accident was in the paper. The woman said she was real sorry. Dad used to come in a lot, Agatha, the way you said he must have."

"To mail packages?"

"Yes," Sandy answered. "She said he'd come a week straight with two or three a day, then she wouldn't see him for a while."

"Did your dad ever talk to her about the packages?" Agatha inquired.

"No. I asked her that, sort of. I asked her if he insured them. When we mail packages for Mom, she always tells us to insure them for the minimum. The woman said Dad didn't. Does that mean they weren't valuable?"

"It may mean he didn't worry about them or maybe that what was inside couldn't be replaced with money. There are some things insurance can't cover."

"She got the mail from Dad's box for us," Kate said. "It's box four-five-one. We should remember that when we come back. It's paid for until the end of October. Here's the mail."

Most of the stuff she handed to Agatha was junk mail addressed to "Boxholder." There was only one envelope addressed to Mr. Ralph Prescott, Box 451, Henderson, New Hampshire. A paste-on address label with the American flag told them it was from Nathan Bush, Stark Lake, Vermont.

"We'll give this to your mother," Agatha said. She looked at her watch. "How about if we put off the visit to the landlady until another day? If your father used this post office, he must have rented the vans and cars nearby. There's a phone booth at the corner, Sandy. You can check the Yellow Pages. Wait a second. Let's see where we are."

Agatha studied the city map of Henderson tucked in the corner of the New Hampshire state map. "We're on Winicook Avenue. Look for car-rental agencies on, let's see, Granite Avenue and High Street. They seem to be the principal streets around here. If that doesn't work, I'll use the telephone tomorrow." Agatha ripped a page out of her notebook. "Here's paper and pen."

Sandy reported that there were only two rental agencies close by, both on Granite Avenue. The first was Ajax Car Rental; the second was Twin City Car and Truck Rental. Ajax, it turned out, didn't rent vans. The Twin City agency did. When Agatha asked the manager if he could remember a customer named Ralph Prescott, he looked at her suspiciously. "The man that died a couple of weeks ago?" he asked.

Agatha nodded. She put her arms around Sandy on one side of her and Kate on the other. "These are his daughters. I'm trying to tidy up the estate for tax purposes," which was true, she figured, in a very remote way. "Mr. Prescott rented cars and vans from you from time to time, did he not?"

"All the time," the man admitted. "Well, not all the time; frequently, you might say. I'm Ted Clancy. I mostly dealt with Ralph. Yeah, he had his own folder." He brought back a manila folder and riffled through a stack of papers. "There must be ten to twelve rentals here, starting last year in early November."

"May we go through them?" Agatha asked. "I'd like to make some notes. Did Mr. Prescott pay with a credit card or check?"

"Cash," Ted Clancy told her, "always cash. He seemed to have a lot of money. Every van rental ran to a couple of hundred dollars. I can't let you take the folder with you. Can you go through it here?"

Agatha nodded. She and the girls sat at a table in the waiting room.

"What are we looking for, Agatha?" Sandy asked.

"We want dates, type of vehicle, and mileage figures. Look," she said, putting the top sheet in front of Sandy, "here you have mileage out and mileage in. The date is here, and the make of car on this line. At the bottom, the charges. You give them to me, and I'll write them in my notebook. When we've finished, I'll read them back from the folder, and you and Kate can double-check."

Clancy was almost right. Ralph Prescott had rented a vehicle from Twin City twelve times between November third and the date on the last sheet, which was, Agatha calculated, three weeks before his death.

"We'll go over these in the Toyota," she said. She thanked Ted Clancy for his help. She wondered if Prescott had been secretive about his trips. "There's a lot of mileage on the trips in the van. Where do you suppose Mr. Prescott went?"

"Up to Canada," Clancy answered. "Somewhere in Quebec. He never said just where. He was starting up an import business, I believe. He had a place down in the Putnam Mill, didn't he? That's the address he gave."

"I believe you're right," Agatha agreed. "Thank you again for your help."

Had her dad intended to have a store in the mill? Kate asked as soon as they left the office. "That would have been neat. We could have visited and helped out, couldn't we, Sandy?"

"Agatha didn't say Dad was going to have a store, did you, Agatha? You were just talking to Mr. Clancy, weren't you?"

"I honestly don't know. It does seem odd he moved to the mill just to be private, although it certainly is that. Maybe your father had the idea that he was going to have a shop there someday. He told you he'd have things straightened around by summer, didn't he?"

"Yes."

"Well, it might have been he was thinking of a place on the first floor. We'll find out, Sandy. I'm just very sorry your dad isn't here to be able to tell you himself."

"An antiques shop, like the one across from where Mom works in Winthrop?"

"Something like that, I suppose," Agatha replied.

"Well, what was he doing in that old apartment?" Kate went on. "And at the post office? And with those cars he was renting? What kind of business was that?"

"It was a kind of mail-order and traveling business, Kate. I'm guessing he was working for someone else."

"The man in the car who hit him?" Sandy asked. "The man Mom says paid his hospital bills? The French Canadian guy?"

So Lydia was talking to her children about Ralph, Agatha noted. That was good. "Perhaps," she said. "Let's see what we have." She turned on the car light and once again went over the figures and dates.

"What was your father doing?" she asked. "Except for November, at the beginning, he rented a van and went to Canada about once a month. He came back and rented a car a couple of times. Then nothing for a while. Then a van, next a car. One long trip and a couple of short trips. Out and around from Henderson, it looks like."

"Maybe up to Stark Lake; right, Agatha?" Kate said. "Let's open the letter."

"No, that is for your mother to do. If it's important, she'll show it to us. She knows what we are up to."

"He was selling antiques he bought in Canada, that's what he was doing," Sandy said. "Isn't that it, Agatha?"

"What kind of antiques, Sandy? Any special kind?"

"Carvings," Sandy and Kate shouted together. "He was selling Eskimo carvings like the ones he gave us."

"Perhaps not exactly like the ones he gave you," Agatha answered. "There aren't enough of those to start a business with. Carvings, yes, Eskimo artifacts. I'm pretty sure we can settle on that. Now, it's home in a hurry. We'll get some subs for you to take home to eat while you do your homework. You can celebrate with Duke. It's been a good day for detectives Sandy and Kate Prescott."

"Lieutenant Bates," Sergeant Trudeau said over the phone, "I'm glad I caught you. I tried off and on the last couple of days without any luck."

Agatha turned out the flame under the teakettle. "I've been out a lot of the time," she answered. "Over in Henderson, as a matter of fact."

"It wasn't anything important, but I wanted to tell you we talked to the night watchman at the Putnam Mill. Actually, he's the watchman at the Dawson Mill, down from the Putnam Mill. He comes over to the Putnam twice a night to check up."

"I know," Agatha replied. "Don Ostel told me about him. What did he have to say?"

"Last Saturday night, more like early Sunday morning, about two o'clock, he walked up to the Putnam Mill. As he headed into the parking lot, a car parked there turned on its lights and roared out into the street. The watchman checked the outside door and all the doors inside. He didn't find anything wrong. He didn't think anything more about it until we talked to him. Kids use the parking lot to drink beer in. Couples sneak in there to park for a while. He's had to call us a couple of times to chase cars away."

"Where do the cars park? It's a big lot," Agatha commented.

"That's it, Lieutenant. The watchman says the car was parked right at the door to the mill. Usually people park in the far corners. He thinks it might have been a big Mercedes."

"Isn't that the kind of car that a witness told Officer Melankamp might have struck Prescott last September?"

"Yes. That's why I thought you might want to know. As far as we're concerned, it doesn't change much of anything, but, still, it *is* a coincidence."

Agatha told Trudeau about her visit to St. Agnes Hospital and Twin City Car and Truck Rental. "Do you think Nurse Drago noticed what kind of car Prescott and his friend drove off in? It didn't occur to me to ask."

"I'll find out for certain," Trudeau promised. "And you say this guy Clancy swears Prescott told him he went up to Canada in the vans he rented?"

"He didn't swear, exactly. It's something Ralph Prescott apparently told him. I studied the map last evening. The mileage from Henderson to the Canadian border and back just about matches the mileage on the rental sheet. He couldn't have gone very far into the country."

"Perhaps you have the makings of a case here, Lieutenant Bates. I'll talk to Fred and the chief. We'll be in touch. Thanks for the information."

Agatha let out a breath of satisfaction. She had them moving at last. She spread her notes over the kitchen table and heated the water again. She half expected Lydia Prescott to call about the letter from Nathan Bush, but there was no call. Toward noon she put on her jacket to scatter fertilizer on the front lawn. Henry had never bothered, she was sure, but Arthur Harper had taken charge of her lawn and he assured her an early spring application of fertilizer was just the thing for a healthy green lawn. He promised to help her cut the grass if it got out of hand.

At two-thirty, Agatha picked up Sandy and Kate at school. "After you run the dog," she said, "why don't we visit Mrs. Cotter at your father's old boardinghouse?"

"Fine with us," said Sandy. "First we have a surprise for you. Shall we tell her, Kate?"

"No way," Kate shouted in Agatha's ear. "We'll show her."

Agatha sat on the hood of the Toyota while the girls raced into the house to deposit their backpacks and let Duke out. They came running back with the puppy snapping at their heels. Kate knelt with the dog alongside the car.

"Sit, Duke," she ordered. "Sit!"

Duke licked Kate in the face with his big tongue. He cocked his ears and panted.

"Sit, Duke, sit!"

Duke's back legs began to twitch and bend. Then he jumped up and put his paws on Kate's shoulders and licked her face again.

"Sit, Duke! Sit this minute," Kate said firmly.

Slowly Duke leaned backward. He sat until Kate gave him a hug. Then he bounded away under the pine trees.

"See, Agatha," Kate said proudly. "He sat for me. He really did. He's the greatest dog there ever was."

"He's my dog, too," Sandy said sharply. "And Mom's.

110

The next trick is my turn. I'm going to teach him to roll over."

"Who's going to teach Duke to come when he's called?" Agatha asked. She had been shouting at the puppy in vain.

"You can teach him that," Sandy said. She trapped Duke and led him back into the mobile home. "Okay, we're ready now."

Mrs. Cotter's boardinghouse was a large, ramshackle house on a side street on the west bank of the Winicook River. Once an elegant Victorian residence, it was now a faded old house on a street of faded, ill-attended old houses. A handmade sign nailed to the porch railing announced rooms for rent.

An elderly woman came to the door. She stared at Agatha and the girls. "I don't rent to children," she said. "I have nothing against them, mind you—I have four of my own—but some of my guests are fragile."

"We don't need a room, thank you," Agatha said kindly. "We only want to talk to you a minute about Ralph Prescott. This is Sandy and this is Kate, his daughters. I'm a friend of theirs, Agatha Bates."

Mrs. Cotter's stern expression relaxed. She sniffled and a tear ran down her cheek. "Oh, my," she exclaimed, "you are Ralph's daughters, are you? You are all he ever talked about. Why, he came over from the mill just a few days before the accident. He said, and these are his very words, 'I'm going to make it, Emily. I'm going to have them with me again.' And then the accident, such an awful thing to happen. Come on in, please."

The living room was worn but comfortable. A vacuum cleaner rested in the middle. "I was cleaning downstairs,"

Mrs. Cotter said. "You're lucky I heard you knocking at the door. I'm so sorry about your father, girls. He was like a son to me the two years he was here. There was nothing he wouldn't do, take out the trash, shovel the walk, fix things, wax the floor. But you could see all the time he wanted his family."

"Was Dad all right?" Sandy asked. "I mean, did he still have his drinking problem?"

Mrs. Cotter admitted that Ralph Prescott did have his problem. Sometimes he had to have help getting back home from the bar he favored. Sometimes she would find a bottle of whiskey in his room, which she confiscated for Ralph's own good. "The stuff was bad for him," she confided, "and he knew it. It was destroying him right in front of my eyes."

"All the time was he drunk?" Kate asked.

"He'd stop for a couple of weeks sometimes, but he couldn't stop for good. When he started again, he tried to make up for lost time. It was terrible. I sent him to my doctor, who said he should go to a special hospital. Ralph didn't have any money for that, and he didn't want to go anyway. It was the accident—the first accident—that saved him. Ralph understood how close he came to getting himself killed. He said he'd never take another drop."

"Then he moved across the river, is that right, Mrs. Cotter?" Agatha asked.

"About a month later, I'd say. Over into the Putnam Mill. He told me he didn't want to go—this was his home—but he needed space. He was going into business with a friend. He came here one day with a tall, well-dressed man. It must have been when he was released from

Saint Agnes. He was still in his old clothes. They went up to Ralph's room."

"You didn't see the man again?"

"No. He may have come—I heard some talking in Ralph's room—but I didn't see him. Within a week, believe it or not, Ralph was a changed man."

"What do you mean?" Sandy asked.

"Your father didn't look after himself, Sandy, while he was here. Whatever money he had he used for his rent and spent the rest at the bar. I tried to feed him as best I could, but he didn't eat the way he should have. He didn't cut his hair and he didn't shave very often. 'Honestly, Ralph,' I'd say, 'you're a mess.' He'd clean himself up for a day or two; then he'd forget. What happened was that he started to look after himself. He bought new clothes, good ones, too, you could see that. He ate regularly, too."

"At the City Line Café?" Kate asked.

Mrs. Cotter looked at Kate, curious. "How did you know that?"

"It's where he used to eat when he married Mom. That's what she said."

"That's nice. I didn't know that. The City Line has been here as long as I have," Mrs. Cotter said. "Anyway, Ralph Prescott was a changed man. When he moved over to the mill, he came back often to see how I was. He always said he was going to make it. He had something to prove. His very words were, 'I have something to prove to my kids.'"

It was Sandy, not the sensitive Kate, who responded to Mrs. Cotter's words. She cried. She held out her hand to Agatha for a tissue. "Why did it have to happen?" she sobbed.

Kate put her arm around Sandy. "It's all right, Sandy. He loved us. That's what he told Mrs. Cotter. That's what matters now, Sandy. He loved us, and he was getting ready to help look after us."

Kate started to sob, too. She put her head in Agatha's lap and shook with sorrow.

Agatha reached out and drew Sandy to her. She wondered if she should keep on pursuing Ralph Prescott and his elusive friend. It looked like a good time to stop.

19

Lydia picked up the letter from her bureau absentmindedly. What was this? A letter to Ralph from someone in Vermont. The girls must have put it there Wednesday night when they came home from Henderson, and she hadn't noticed it yesterday morning. They were so busy playing with Duke they had forgotten to remind her. Duke was now stretched out on the rag rug in her room, nose resting between his enormous front paws, watching her with his two odd eyes.

What a difference he had made in their lives. She bent down to scratch Duke behind his ears. He made that funny noise in his throat to tell her how good it felt.

Lydia made a mental note to speak with Arthur Harper about the insurance. She realized Agatha and Harper had advised her to wait, but what was the point of it? She had no intention of putting herself and the girls through the anguish of dredging up poor Ralph's past. He was gone and that was the end of it. The girls insisted that he had reformed, but he had reformed before, she remembered, only to go back to the bottle after a couple of months. If Mr. Harper could settle for twenty thousand, it would take care of a car and maybe an addition to the house.

With that thought, Lydia felt happy as she poured her last cup of coffee and sat down at the counter, the envelope in her hand. Who was Nathan Bush? Where was Stark Lake? She had never heard of it. She opened the envelope.

"Dear Mr. Prescott," Lydia read from the single sheet of paper. "I am writing about the Eskimo piece I bought in February. I like it very much. However, I have noticed a crack at the base. It must have been there when I purchased it, and I failed to notice. When you come this way again, could you drop by and take a look? It may need a replacement. We can discuss that. Six hundred dollars is a bit much to pay for a damaged piece. Thank you. Nathan Bush."

Lydia puzzled over what she had read. It was difficult, very difficult, for her to think of Ralph as a dealer in Eskimo carvings. True, Agatha had said something to that effect, and the girls had assured her all winter that Ralph was in business. Still, Ralph knew nothing about such things. Were they stolen, as Agatha had suggested? She rejected that thought once again. He must have been a partner, as Ostel said. The girls said he had gone to Canada in a van once a month. It was very strange.

The thing to do was to show Agatha the letter. She heard Peggy's wreck of a car outside. Lydia looked at her watch. They had time to drop the letter off at Agatha's place. She hustled into her coat, gave Duke a good-bye pat, and ran to the car.

"I can't stay," she told Agatha at the door. "We have to start setting up the tables by eleven. Here's the letter the

116

girls brought home. I didn't notice it until this morning. You were right. Ralph was in some kind of business. I'll see you." Lydia headed back to the car.

Agatha scanned the letter. "Wait a minute, Lydia," she called. "May I take Kate and Sandy to Stark Lake, wherever that is, tomorrow?"

"Sure, they'll love that. Did they tell you next week is school vacation week? They could go then, too. We have to rush. If you see Mr. Harper, tell him I'd like to talk to him this weekend if that's all right. It's about the insurance."

Agatha nodded and went inside. Where was Stark Lake? she wondered. She opened her map on the table. Why, it wasn't so for after all, not more than fifty miles northwest from Wingate on Route 30. Maybe the puppy could go along, too. She put Nathan Bush's letter in her purse along with her notes. It was time to have another talk with Malcolm Torbert.

Chief Torbert listened without comment as Agatha reported on her week's activities. When she finished, he said, "Well, it does seem to go in a straight line, Deputy Bates. Trudeau must be interested by now. He's going to talk to Melankamp, is he? Fred is a reasonable man."

"If they discover there's a Mercedes in Prescott's life, they may get busy. I'm convinced it was the man who paid Prescott's bill. They were into something after that. He was at the bridge that night. He must have been. Then he came back later to try to collect the carvings."

"He came back to look for something else, didn't he, Agatha?"

"What do you mean, Malcolm?"

"You've already said Prescott probably kept his papers in one of those boxes. There must have been things there that his silent partner wanted. Bankbooks, receipts, addresses, correspondence, whatever."

"That's true. I've thought of making the rounds of banks, but that's police work. It's probably useless, anyway. Prescott did his business in cash. The girls received cash. He probably paid Lydia's phone bill with a countercheck or money order."

"Why do you reckon he didn't have his own phone? Either he didn't want to pay income taxes or he didn't want to leave a trail. It's likely the Canadian had an account somewhere that Prescott deposited the receipts in."

"He didn't have a phone for the same reason he didn't have a bank account," Agatha replied. "Part of his business Prescott kept private. Trudeau can get records for that phone in the factory if he wants to."

"But Prescott went to the post office and car agencies."

"Yes, he did. He was open about that. He made no effort to hide what he was doing. The letter proves that. But he didn't talk about his partner."

"What you are saying, Agatha, is that Prescott had a silent partner who insisted on staying in the shadows. A partner who was peddling Eskimo sculptures."

"Antiques and artifacts. You're not going to purchase a thousand-year-old carving for six hundred dollars, Malcolm."

"I don't know anything about it, but you're probably right. These days you don't even get much bubble gum for six hundred bucks. That still doesn't explain anything."

"I think it does. Most countries have very strict laws about exporting historical materials. Even within the country, you sometimes have to have government approval to sell them. Dr. Langhorne will verify that."

"You mean I can't sell my collection of arrowheads, Agatha?" Torbert laughed. "I have a stone ax head, too, that I found by the pond when I was a kid."

"Take that up with Mavis Langhorne, Malcolm. Maybe she'll trade you a dog for your collection, a bloodhound to help you in your work. Mavis is an expert on dogs."

"Maybe I will. What you suppose is that a Canadian antiques dealer ran into Ralph Prescott one night in his Mercedes. He felt bad about it, not bad enough to go to the police, but bad enough to visit Ralph in the hospital, find out who or what he was, and pay his bill. Then he made Ralph his business partner right off. That sounds farfetched to me," Torbert observed.

"To me, too, Malcolm. That's where I have trouble. But it happened—for reasons we don't know yet. One good reason we can guess at. If the stranger was peddling illegal objects, which, let's say for a moment, were stolen, he was safer having Ralph Prescott transport them across the border than doing it himself. And delivering them, too."

"You may be right, Agatha. They found a nice quiet place in the mill, paid a year's rent in advance—in cash, if you're right. New clothes for Ralph and a bit of furniture."

"Around the first of November, his new friend brought a shipment of carvings down to Ralph, all new ones, I think, or reproductions, and a list of addresses. Ralph took to the road. That seems to be what the car records show. He probably mailed some, too, to farther points. After that, Ralph went to Canada to pick up the stuff."

"Just across the border, according to you, Agatha," Torbert continued. "You're going to tell me he was met somewhere by the stranger, aren't you? Prescott wasn't to find out where the stranger lived."

119

"Malcolm, you should be a detective, too."

"Next, you are going to tell me Ralph Prescott rented a van to carry boxes of apples back across the border, and the carvings were tucked in with apples."

"You have it, Chief Torbert. Somehow the man convinced poor Ralph it was better to avoid trouble with the customs people because there was a heavy import fee on Eskimo carvings or something like that. Nothing very serious, but something to be avoided."

"The purpose of this elaborate game was to slip some expensive antiquities into the country?"

"I don't know enough about Eskimo artifacts to answer your question, but I do suspect that was the purpose of the game. But I'm pretty certain about one thing."

"Which is?"

"That Ralph Prescott didn't know any more about his business partner than we do."

"You reckon you can find out, don't you, Agatha?" Torbert asked with a smile.

"I do indeed. Ralph Prescott probably didn't want to. He had something more important to think about: his future. He didn't ask any questions. The stranger told Ralph Prescott some things he could accept, and, for a while at least, Ralph believed, and did what he was told. Until he came upon the polar bear and the knife. That was a fatal discovery for Ralph, I think. The second time the stranger hit Ralph, it was for good."

Torbert whistled with astonishment. "You have it all figured out, don't you? Do you know what, Deputy Bates?"

"What, Malcolm?"

"If I were that Canadian, I wouldn't want you after me."

"We'll see, Chief Torbert, we'll see."

20

Taking the puppy along in the car on an all-day trip wasn't the greatest idea she had ever had, Agatha Bates decided. Not that she wasn't prepared. She had tucked two plastic trash bags over the backseat and stretched two beach towels over them. Duke seemed happy enough. He jumped right in, sniffed the beach towels, and stretched out with his head on Kate's lap.

"He's really housebroken," Sandy assured Agatha. "Aunt Peggy came over early yesterday morning, Mom said, and took him for a ride to the pond and back. They said it was a dry run for today."

Aunt Peggy has a sense of humor, Agatha thought. The trouble, when it came, wasn't with the housebroken Duke. It was with the carsick Duke. Halfway to Stark Lake, Duke lifted his head, choked a couple of times, and threw up his breakfast in Kate's lap.

Agatha pulled the Toyota to the side of the road. Duke jumped out, tail between his legs, looking worried and ashamed. Kate was on the edge of tears. "You stupid dog," she shouted to Duke. "Look what you've done to my new jeans. What am I going to do, Agatha?"

"It's not Duke's fault, Kate," Agatha replied, wiping the breakfast off Kate's jeans with a fistful of tissues. "My daughter Sarah couldn't ride in a car for half an hour straight. We had to stop and let her walk around the car."

"I found a stream down in the woods," Sandy called. "Come on, Kate. I'll wash off your jeans down here. Bring a towel to wrap around you. You can sit in the car when we get there."

"Bring the jeans back to me," Agatha ordered, "and I'll put them in front of the heater and turn it up all the way. They'll dry fast. We'll stop and have an early lunch in the car, so they'll have more time to dry."

"What about Duke?" Kate asked. "What if he isn't really housebroken? I've taken one of his towels."

"You must explain his responsibilities to him, Kate. He looks like a smart dog. Tell him to let us know if he wants to get out."

For the rest of the trip to Stark Lake, Duke sat up on his side of the backseat, his nose to the window Agatha had cracked open. Once, he leaned over to lick Kate in the face to tell her he was really sorry.

The jeans *were* dry when they located Nathan Bush's house, exactly where he had told Agatha she could find him. It was a large, modern structure at the head of a meadow that stretched down to a beach.

"Mr. Bush must be a millionaire," Sandy said. "Look at the size of that house. And he has his own private beach. Dad must have been in a good business."

"We'll soon see," Agatha said. "Hold Duke's leash tight. Some people aren't too fond of dogs."

Nathan Bush turned out to be very fond of dogs. He knew all about Newfoundlands. He used to have one, he told Sandy and Kate, named Lumberjack, who went swimming every day in the lake when it wasn't frozen over.

"We'll take Duke down in a bit to see if he's a real water dog. You've brought his beach towel, good. In the meantime, come on in."

Mr. Bush explained that he was alone. His wife was a commercial artist, he said, who spent a good deal of time in New York. He didn't say what he did. Sandy was probably right, Agatha thought. Bush *was* a millionaire, or close to it.

Inside, he showed them the piece he had written Ralph Prescott about. It was a heavy, square carving, in black soapstone, of an Inuit hunter with a knife in his hand, fighting a polar bear. It didn't look as thought the hunter was going to win. At the base, Bush pointed to a crack or a deep scratch, Agatha couldn't be sure which.

"Soapstone is quite soft. This may be where the carver's knife slipped, or it may be a crack or a scratch. I really can't tell. I'm sorry to hear your father died," Bush said to the girls. "If I had known, I wouldn't have written the letter. It's not a matter of great importance."

"Dad would have fixed it for you, maybe, or brought you a new one," Kate said. "He told us he was a good businessman, didn't he, Sandy?"

Sandy agreed. "We can give the money back to you when we get Dad's insurance—can't we, Agatha? Mom would want us to do that. It's six hundred dollars, isn't it?"

"I wouldn't hear of it," Bush said. "I'll put it back on the shelf with the others. No one will notice, and I'll forget about it. I didn't have Mr. Campeau's address, or I would have dealt directly with him."

"Mr. Campeau?" Agatha said. "He sold you the piece? I thought it was Mr. Prescott."

"Both, really, I suppose. Mr. Campeau came by the house at the end of the summer. He had heard, I'm not sure how, that I have a small collection of carvings. He asked if I was still interested in Eskimo sculpture."

"He was a dealer?" Agatha asked.

"He said he was, up in Quebec province somewhere. I don't think he said where. I may have bought something from him years ago when I was on vacation in Canada. I can't remember. Or he may have gotten my address from *Eskimo Arts*. That's a magazine I used to subscribe to. Anyway, he knew who I was."

"But he didn't have this piece with him?"

"No, no. He had only a couple of sculptures in the car. He had a large folder of photographs, with sizes, origins, and certification. Two hundred or more, I'd say. He told me he was selling his collection, he was in another line of business. He wanted to sell in this country, since the Canadian dollar was so weak. He had some really lovely pieces."

"Were they expensive?" Sandy asked.

"Not too expensive, but certainly not as cheap as they used to be. They must have cost from three hundred to two thousand dollars each. Campeau said the price was increasing about ten percent a year. I believe him. Anyway, I selected this piece. It wasn't like anything I had. He promised to deliver it on his next trip. But it was your dad who brought it to me," Bush told Sandy and Kate. "He said he was Mr. Campeau's American partner. Later, I discovered this crack or scratch."

"Could we see the rest of your collection?" Sandy asked.

"Come into the study. They are in a cabinet I had made for them. Campeau said I had made a good purchase on several of them. They are quite valuable now."

"How valuable?" Kate asked.

"Oh, I don't know, maybe a thousand dollars or more. I probably only paid fifty dollars for them. But that was fifteen years ago. Everything increases in value these days, if you keep it long enough. They aren't old, you understand, just valuable. The Inuit aren't making as many sculptures as they used to and there are more people who want them."

"Dad gave us two," Kate said. "Agatha says they are priceless. But they aren't like yours. Ours are ivory, aren't they, Agatha?"

"Ivory, that's great," Bush said. "They don't work in ivory much anymore. Soapstone is easier and cheaper for them to use. I'd like to see your pieces the next time you come by."

While she admired Nathan Bush's collection, Agatha asked. "You don't have any idea of Mr. Campeau's address? Or a first name? I am trying to help straighten out Mr. Prescott's affairs. It seems to have been an informal partnership. I can't locate an address for him."

"That's odd," Bush agreed. "Mr. Prescott gave me a receipt for the carving I purchased. That's how I got in touch with him."

"Apparently Mr. Prescott kept his records in a cardboard box. After his death it must have been thrown out accidentally. No one seems to know. Mr. Harper, that's Mrs. Prescott's attorney, is quite concerned about estate and income taxes."

"I understand, but I'm no use to you. Campeau's first

name may have been Robert. He shouldn't be hard to find if he was a dealer in Quebec. He found me easily enough."

"I'm sure it won't be difficult. Mr. Harper will locate him. A tall man, sixty or so, with glasses?"

"That's him, all right."

"I thought it would be," Agatha remarked. "Probably driving his Mercedes, wasn't he? Mr. Prescott told Kate and Sandy his partner drove a big expensive Mercedes." Agatha hoped Kate would not interrupt to question that little lie. But Kate wasn't listening. She was studying the soapstone sculptures.

"A big one is right," Bush said with admiration. "It made my two-eighty look like a compact. You have the right man. Well, if you two girls are ready, let's go see if Duke is a water dog. Bring a towel."

Duke was a water dog. He charged straight out into Stark Lake. It took him about a minute to learn to use his paws and keep his head above water. Then he settled in to retrieve the sticks Sandy and Kate threw into the lake.

As they got into the Toyota, a question flashed through Agatha's mind. She put her head out the car window. "Tell me, Mr. Bush. Did Mr. Campeau offer you any old carvings, authentic antiquities?"

"Funny that you should ask. He did. He said he had another folder of very old pieces. They were terribly expensive, he said. I told him I wasn't a serious collector. He said he understood. I didn't see the folder."

"Thank you, Mr. Bush," Agatha said. "You have been very kind."

21

It was time to talk to Dr. Langhorne's expert. Le Maître, that was his name. She would ask Mavis to give him a call. We'll need some sort of introduction, Agatha told herself. We can't go barging up there with thousand-year-old carvings and a crazy story about birthday presents.

And I'll have to bring Trudeau up to date, she thought. Had Nurse Drago remembered a fancy car? That no longer mattered so much, but it might be important. Nathan Bush had established the presence of a tall, well-dressed dealer in Eskimo art, calling himself Campeau and driving a Mercedes. I will bring everything up to date, she decided. If there is ever a case, it will have to be Trudeau's.

But, first things first. Agatha drove to Mavis Langhorne's cabin to ask if she would call Le Maître to explain their visit. Mavis said she would be delighted if Agatha would take her back to use Agatha's phone. "I ought to have a phone," she declared, "in case there's an emergency for one of the dogs, but the fact is I don't want a phone to start controlling my life. At the museum, I spent half the day on

127

the telephone. Imagine what a waste of my time. Don't you feel, Agatha, you rely on it more than you should?"

"No," Agatha replied. "No one ever calls me. I wish it would ring every once in a while."

"Then you should certainly get rid of it. Why pay for something you don't use?"

"And my car, too?" Agatha asked. "I don't use it much—at least I didn't until we found the carvings."

"No, no, keep your car." Mavis laughed. "I may need you to take one of the dogs to the vet's someday. You know, I've been thinking about these two carvings. It's none of my business, but I'd bet they were stolen. There's a big business in stolen artifacts. No one knows how big because no one talks about it. We were robbed twice at the museum while I was there. The first time we got the stuff back. The guy had already sold a couple of pieces. The second time, not a trace. People who buy them don't show them off. They just want them for themselves. They'll pay tens of thousands for a good Maya or Inca relic, probably more for an old Eskimo artifact, because there aren't so many. Le Maître will tell you that."

Mavis Langhorne started speaking in French as soon as the call went through. She chatted fluently for several minutes before hanging up with the only words Agatha could understand: "Merci beaucoup, professeur."

"Doesn't Le Maître speak English?" Agatha asked, worried about how she and the girls could converse with the great man.

"Of course he does, perfectly. He was talking in English while I was trying to talk in French. We wanted to be professional. It always gives you an advantage to be able to talk to a foreigner in his or her language. I can get along

128

pretty well in French or Spanish. I don't need anything else."

"Will he see us?"

"He certainly will. I told him you had come into possession—I didn't say how—of a couple of Dorset Culture pieces that he might be familiar with. He expects you next Friday. You said Kate and Sandy had next week free, is that right? Anyway, call him up when you get to Quebec."

"Friday is fine," Agatha said. They could leave on Wednesday, have Thursday for a tour of the city, and come home Friday afternoon. Lydia Prescott was pleased to have the girls make the trip. And Sandy was excited. She had begun studying French in the seventh grade. She was busy teaching Kate the words she had learned.

"One thing more, Agatha," Mavis said. "It's none of my business, but I wouldn't take those carvings with me. I don't know whom they belong to, but I suspect Le Maître won't allow you to bring them back until the Canadian authorities give you permission. You'd better show him photographs. Promise him the carvings later, if you need them here for whatever you are up to."

"But . . ." Agatha protested.

"I can photograph them for you. I have the equipment in the basement. I use it for my own research. I can give you photographs as good as the carvings, maybe better. I'll blow them up. That's all Le Maître needs. The girls understand they can't keep them, don't they?"

"Yes. I told them that. They don't care much. Perhaps Le Maître will help them pick out some modern ones, which they like better. Yesterday we saw some lovely sculptures that a collector in Vermont had. The girls like birds and seals, they decided."

129

"Give me a ride back, and I'll get to work on the photographs," Dr. Langhorne said. "I'll have them ready for you by Tuesday."

Now, sitting at her desk, Agatha prepared a report for Trudeau, which she would send him in the morning. She turned over in her head what she had learned about Ralph Prescott's life since the evening late last September when he was struck by a Mercedes, presumably driven by a Canadian handicraft dealer calling himself Campeau. As a result of that chance encounter, Prescott had been miraculously cured of his alcoholism. How? Or better, by whom? The answer was obvious. By Campeau.

Why? Probably Campeau's feelings of guilt.

What had possessed Campeau to take the derelict—a reformed derelict, perhaps—into the Eskimo carving business? Not guilt and not a feeling of responsibility, either, Agatha was sure of that. Campeau had not acquired a Mercedes and an expensive collection of artifacts by taking derelicts into his business.

Something had occurred to Campeau, after—maybe even before—he rescued Prescott from St. Agnes Hospital. He needed something for himself, not for Ralph Prescott.

What did he need? An American distributor? Perhaps. An innocent, unquestioning American distributor? Probably.

Why? It was no great burden, so far as Agatha could see, for Campeau to drive down from Quebec to deliver the carvings once a month or so. Or let someone else do it. Or send them by mail. Perhaps the carvings were fragile. No. Prescott mailed them, apparently. Customs inspections? That was a possibility, perhaps. There were restrictions on

130

exporting works of art. She would ask Le Maître. A partner could take care of that, she supposed.

But a partner like Ralph Prescott, a bum who knew nothing about what he was delivering?

That was the point, wasn't it? Agatha realized with absolute certainty. It was not that Prescott could be trusted or not trusted. What was important was that he could be used.

For delivering modern carvings, like those in Nathan Bush's collection? No, indeed. Campeau saw Ralph Prescott as the courier for Inuit sculptures, which, according to Mavis, could be worth tens of thousands of American dollars. Campeau would sell these antiquities discreetly and have Ralph deliver them. And he could let Ralph sell the modern ones on commission.

For reasons as yet unknown, Campeau did not dare deliver the old pieces himself. Apparently, he did not want to attempt to carry them across the border. That was Ralph's job.

How was it done? The carvings, new and old, were to be smuggled in by a phony apple dealer named Ralph Prescott. Campeau must have told Prescott some acceptable story about export restrictions on Eskimo sculpture, or perhaps exchange difficulties, something that didn't seem too illegal to Campeau's grateful new partner.

Prescott brought in the carvings and delivered them or mailed them as Campeau instructed. He took orders for the pieces Campeau had in the big folder. Once a month, at a specified time, Campeau called Prescott at the pay phone. A meeting was arranged and Ralph drove north in his van. If he suspected anything strange about his partner's behavior, Ralph Prescott remained silent.

He was happy. More than that, he was proud of his suc-

131

cess. Agatha could imagine Lydia's husband in his new clothes—which Campeau must have selected for him—setting out to deliver or sell Eskimo art. He told the girls that he would have his business under control—something like that—by summer. He had dreams of opening a shop on the first floor, Agatha guessed. Campeau must have encouraged him. Ralph was going to have his family back.

What happened to his rosy future? Suddenly, in mid-March, Ralph Prescott took out a whopping insurance policy. And . . . and what? What a fool I am, Agatha muttered to herself. She took Prescott's key ring from the desk drawer. One key for the apartment, one key she had supposed was to the front door of the mill. A little key to a trunk or metal box or something like that.

She went to the kitchen. Tom was curled up in her chair. Agatha shooed him away and sat down to dial Don Ostel's number.

"Tell me, Don, when did Ralph put that new lock on his apartment?"

"Last month, I'm pretty sure. He had a locksmith install it."

"You said he didn't give you a key. Do you have a key to the lock that was there before?"

"Sure. I have keys to all the studios on the second floor."

Agatha held the keys in front of her. "Describe it as best you can."

Ostel did as she asked. The second key, which she had assumed was the key to the mill's main door, was the one to the old apartment lock. Prescott had not discarded it. But where was the key to the main door? In one place only: Campeau's pocket.

In the shipment that Ralph Prescott brought down from

132

Canada in early March, Campeau must have put the first antiques he trusted his American partner to deliver. He figured that Ralph was now sufficiently trained to follow the routine. The bear and the knife were to be delivered, or mailed, the same as the other sculptures.

For reasons that Agatha could only guess at, Prescott sensed the two antiques were different. Perhaps he had begun, in anticipation of having his own shop, to make a study of Inuit art. He did not deliver the two precious carvings. His partner may have made a mistake. He waited for the end-of-the-month phone call.

As he waited, Ralph Prescott must have thought hard about Campeau's secretive behavior. Maybe it wasn't a mistake. He became afraid. He put a new lock on the door. He wrapped the carvings in birthday paper and put them in a clothes box. The more he thought about his powerful, decisive partner, the more concerned he became. He took out the life insurance policy.

When the call came, Prescott asked Campeau to come to Henderson. They met on the bridge, not in the apartment. Ralph told him his suspicions. He must have told him more than he should have.

Either they fought and Ralph slipped or Campeau knocked Ralph senseless. He went through Ralph's pockets. He took the keys, cleaned out the wallet and put it back. Then he pushed Prescott down the slope, into the torrents of the Winicook River.

He went to the apartment, made a hurried search for the carvings, and left with the box that held Prescott's records. He took with him the second key to the new lock and the front-door key. Ralph's key chain he threw on the chair. He left the door open.

133

There had to be a fourth box, which Campeau carried off, Agatha wrote in her report to Trudeau. Later, when Campeau figured it was safe, he returned and searched the apartment thoroughly for the two carvings. He probably remembered the birthday packages he had seen earlier. He took the rest of Prescott's boxes to examine at his leisure. But he didn't find the knife and the polar bear.

Agatha felt a chill run through her. There was only one logical place left for Campeau to look. Sooner or later, he would come looking—not in Henderson, but in Wingate, at the Prescotts' lonely mobile home in the pine grove.

22

When Agatha came Wednesday morning to pick up Sandy and Kate, Lydia told her that she was taking Duke to Peggy's house in Winthrop, where she could walk him during her afternoon break.

"The girls are as excited as can be," she said. "They haven't been anywhere since we moved here, except for a school trip to Boston. We certainly didn't go anywhere when we lived in Henderson, I can tell you. The only thing is, they don't want to leave that silly dog. Look at the three of them."

Kate and Sandy had their arms around Duke, who was squirming to get away. They told him how much they were going to miss him and promised to bring him some big Canadian bones. Duke worked himself loose and ran down the lane to the turnaround beyond the two empty trailers. He barked at the girls to come chase him.

"He's a great watchdog," Lydia went on. "He sleeps behind the counter now, on the linoleum. It's cooler there than on the carpet in Kate's room. Last night late I heard him growl. He went to the door and barked. I got up to calm him down. It was only a car turning around down beyond the trailers. Some kids, probably. But Duke heard them, sure enough."

"Did you see the car?" Agatha asked.

"I looked out the window. It was dark, but I think it was big. It went out slowly, past the houses back to the road. Duke barked again as it passed. Cars come down here once in a while at night. I feel better now that we have a phone and a dog. At New Year's, there was a party at the turn-around. I was able to call the police station, and Parker MacDonald, the deputy, drove out and chased them away."

"I was going to ask you to spend the nights at your sister's while we are away," Agatha said. "And at my house, you and the girls, when we come back on Friday."

"That's silly," Lydia said. "I have Duke here. Good heavens, the girls are here at night until I get home from work. I wouldn't leave them here unless I felt they were safe. I'll be all right."

"Please do as I ask," Agatha said firmly. "I have a good idea your husband was drowned by a man looking for two ivory carvings. That is the only reasonable explanation for his death, I'm afraid. I have told the police in Henderson what I think. That man will come here sooner or later—sooner, I believe—looking for those birthday presents. I plan to be ready when he shows up. Stay away from here. I'll ask Torbert to keep an eye on the place for you."

"I guess I should be afraid, but after Kate's kidnapping I doubt I'll ever be able to be afraid again. Poor Ralph. He was bound to come to a bad end. Sure, I'll stay at Peggy's."

Agatha said nothing. It seemed to her that Ralph had

136

died a better death than Lydia supposed. But how do you measure how someone dies? She asked Lydia if she could use her phone.

"I'll do that, Agatha," Torbert said. "Your friend Trudeau just called here. He couldn't get you at the house. He said you were probably on your way to Quebec. He told me about your report. They're back on the case. Is there anything else I can do?"

"Yes, but it can wait. I'll call you when we get back."

"Fine. Trudeau said that when he went to the Henderson town library to find out about Eskimo art, he discovered Ralph Prescott had been there before him."

"In March?" Agatha asked.

"In March, he said," Torbert replied. "Is there anything you don't already know, Agatha?"

"A great deal, Malcolm, but I'm working on it. I figure I'll find out pretty soon."

"Well, have a good trip, Deputy Bates. Take care of yourself."

Agatha had found the guidebook to Quebec that she and Henry had used when they took the children to Canada years ago. "The city is almost four hundred years old," she told Sandy and Kate. "It started out as a fur-trading center on the Saint Lawrence River. The British and the French fought over it for a hundred years before the British took possession."

"But they still speak French, don't they?" Sandy asked. "That's what my teacher, Miss Engel, said. She says it is the most beautiful city in North America."

"She may be right," Agatha admitted. "Some people say

137

Boston, others say San Francisco. I've been to Quebec once. We spent almost a week, as I remember, poking around the narrow streets and pacing off the battleground where the British general, Wolfe, did battle with the French general on what they called the Plains of Abraham. Neither one survived. My daughter Sarah bought a small green seal carved out of soapstone. I wonder if she still has it."

Agatha remembered staying at the huge hotel, the Frontenac, fashioned like a French chateau. This time Agatha had found a small hotel, highly rated in her old guidebook, right on the city square. The clerk told her, when she called to reserve the rooms, it was on the second floor, above one of the city's best restaurants.

"Tomorrow," she continued, "we will have a tour in a horse carriage. In the afternoon we will use our legs. Don't be disappointed if it rains. My book says April is not the best month to visit."

"I don't care," Kate said. "We have our parkas and lots of dry clothes. I'm going to buy some patches for my new denim jacket. When do we see the professor?"

"Friday morning. We'll take you home to Duke Friday afternoon. You'll be staying with me for a few days. Your mother, too."

"Why?" Kate demanded. "What about Duke?"

"Duke, too. He can make friends with Tom. I think you'll be safer at my house in case Mr. Campeau comes looking for those carvings. We'll have Chief Torbert and Parker MacDonald right down the street."

"You think he pushed Dad, don't you, Agatha?" Sandy said. "That makes him dangerous. Do you have a gun?"

"I do, but I have never used it, and I don't intend to start

138

now. What Mr. Campeau is after are the carvings. He will want to get them without any trouble."

"Are they his?"

"I doubt it. I don't know where he got them, but they mean a lot to him. We'll see what he says if he shows up."

"Agatha," Kate asked, "does that mean maybe we'll get all of Dad's insurance?"

"I hope so," Agatha replied. "He meant for you to have it. Now, tell me what you are going to buy with the money your dad sent you for your mother's presents."

"We haven't decided. We'll find something really nice."

"And for Duke? I heard you promise him something."

"Duke is getting a big leather bone like I saw on television," Kate answered. "It's over a foot long."

"We'll shop tomorrow afternoon on our walking tour," Agatha promised. "Relax now. It's a long trip, most of it quite boring, I'm sure, this time of year. There are sandwiches and soft drinks in the picnic basket. Help yourself. We'll stop along the way for afternoon snacks."

Agatha snapped on her sunglasses and turned the radio to some music the girls would accept. She felt good. Malcolm Torbert was right. "Once a cop, Agatha," he told her, "always a cop."

139

23

Sandy studied the little restaurant. She counted the tables, twelve in all. She couldn't be sure why, but Le Coq d'Argent *was* an elegant restaurant. The thick menu had a silver rooster emblazoned on the cover. There were fresh flowers on the starched white tablecloth, and heavy silver and shiny starched napkins. The only restaurant she and Kate had eaten in before was the City Line Café. She had looked inside the Winthrop House, where Mom worked. It wasn't the same. It was big and elegant. The Silver Rooster was small and elegant. She felt out of place.

The menu was all in French. She was able to translate a few of the words for Kate and Agatha, but she really had to rely on the headwaiter. He urged them to have a specialty of the restaurant, a heavy onion soup with cheese. Agatha agreed, but Kate turned up her nose, and she and Sandy settled for a bean soup and roast beef with funny little potatoes and a fancy salad with things in it that Sandy did not recognize. They all agreed on *gâteau* for dessert. *Gâteau* was supposed to mean some kind of cake. Sandy hoped it was one of those she saw on a cart a waiter in a tuxedo was pushing to the tables for customers to select from.

Kate, too, was lost in admiration. She told Agatha that she had seen fancy restaurants that were supposed to be French on television. They weren't like this, she whispered. "I like this one better."

"The guidebook says it is one of the best restaurants in Quebec," Agatha assured her. "It is very typical, they say." Agatha was equally impressed. She admired the dark wood panels along the walls and the heavy oil paintings of scenes of the ancient city.

For herself she had ordered half a bottle of the wine that the wine waiter had recommended. She sipped it slowly, trying to answer the girls' questions as best she could. The fact was, she realized, that except for her family's visit to Canada many years ago, she was as innocent as Kate and Sandy of faraway places. She and Henry had promised themselves a summer in Europe when she retired, but it was another of the promises they'd made to each other that they weren't able to keep. She felt cheated, the same way, probably, that Lydia Prescott must feel cheated by the hard life an early marriage to Ralph Prescott had forced upon her.

Lydia would have the girls' insurance eventually, Agatha was convinced, if she could bring herself to wait. The mysterious Campeau could testify to what really happened to Ralph Prescott. Check that, she thought. Maybe the mysterious Campeau *could be persuaded* to testify, if he came to collect the ivory carvings.

"Do you think Mom will like her presents?" Kate was asking.

"Who wouldn't like them?" she replied. "I'm green with

141

envy myself." Kate had picked out a soft yellow sweater from Scotland, and in an out-of-the-way little shop Sandy had come across a beautiful handmade cashmere shawl. Agatha had been somewhat surprised at their instinctive good taste. Even the patches Kate bought for her jacket were tasteful, compared to the garish ones she could have chosen.

And Sandy had found a small green soapstone seal rather like Sarah's for her bureau. Agatha was shocked at the price. She lent Sandy the money to make up the difference between the cost and what Sandy had. Their father *had* been in a good business. She wondered what commission Campeau had paid his partner. Whatever it was, it must have seemed like a small fortune to the impoverished Prescott.

Professor Le Maître was waiting for them in his office beyond the courtyard of an old granite university building. "This used to be a seminary," he explained, "before it became a university, too. Most of the university had to move to a new site in Sainte Foy some years ago. I was able to insist on staying here with my little museum. I have retired now, but, as you see, I am still here."

Le Maître was a jolly little bald man with dark horn-rimmed glasses and a thin mustache. He wore a black suit. A thick gold watch chain hung from one vest pocket to another. He looked across the desk at his visitors.

"What do you have for me?" he asked. "Dr. Langhorne wasn't specific. She just said a couple of carvings that perhaps went back to the Dorset period. Is that correct?"

"That is for you to tell us," Agatha replied. "Dr. Langhorne assured us you would have the answer. She made these photographs."

Le Maître's sharp eyes scanned the photographs, one after the other. He handed them back to Agatha. "At last," he exclaimed, "they have shown up. I told the police they would, sooner or later. May I ask where you obtained these?"

"They are our birthday presents," Kate said. "The bear is mine. Sandy got the knife."

The professor was incredulous. "Birthday presents? *Mon dieu,* that is impossible. Do you know what these are?"

"Sure we do. They're made of ivory. Agatha says they're very old and are worth a lot."

"Mrs. Bates is right," Le Maître said. "These are national treasures. They belong to the Canadian government. You must give them back. Do you have them with you, by any chance?"

"You may have them back when Agatha is through with them," Sandy told him. "Agatha warned us that we couldn't keep them. Anyway, we don't like them all that much. We like these better." She took her little green seal from her jacket pocket. She handed it to Le Maître.

He smiled. "This is very nice. Do you know, Sandy, deep down, I like these new carvings better, too. Maybe we can make a trade. I have some very fine carvings, not too old, but authentic Inuit carvings. Would you and your sister consider an exchange?"

"It's okay with me," Sandy said. "How about you, Kate?"

"I think I'd like a bird if you have one," Kate answered.

"A bird it is. I have some lovely owl sculptures. We'll see them in a minute."

143

He turned to Agatha. "Of course, you already know something about these two carvings. Dr. Langhorne was right. They are early Dorset. I authenticated them for the museum many years ago when they were putting together their collection of ancient Eskimo artifacts. They are far and away the very finest ivory pieces they had. It was a national tragedy when they were all stolen."

"Yes," Agatha agreed. "I had to assume they were stolen when Dr. Langhorne told me what she knew about them." She told Le Maître the details of how they came to be in the possession of Kate and Sandy. She explained that their father had recently died in a fall, and they were anxious to locate his elusive Canadian partner, presumably a dealer in Eskimo artifacts.

"Properly speaking, we should say Inuit, Mrs. Bates," Le Maître corrected her. "Most people say Eskimo, so you are forgiven. What you have are Inuit carvings from an early cultural period we call Dorset, situated mainly in the area of Hudson Bay."

Sandy listened intently. So far no one had actually told her how old the carvings were. She decided to ask. "Exactly how old are they, sir? And not that it matters, but Kate and I are curious: How much are they worth? Can you tell us?"

"How old are they? Give or take a hundred years, they are eighteen hundred years old. How much are they worth? Well, to us Canadians, they are priceless. They were carved by the first Canadians, who called themselves the People. They were here thousands of years before we French and English showed up. Still, we regard them as part of *our* history, too. In dollars, you want to know. I can only estimate. Fifty thousand for the bear, perhaps more. I cannot say. A little less for the knife, perhaps. The whole collection was insured over twenty years ago for two million dollars. I believe the reward is still in effect. I will see."

"Reward?" Agatha asked. "Who offered the reward?"

"The insurance company *and* the government. You see, Mrs. Bates, they were stolen—all the best sculptures—from a new museum of indigenous art in Montreal twelve years or so ago. It was the heart of the collection, which told us the thief must have been an expert as well as a crook. We are convinced it was a dealer. The pieces had to begin to show up sooner or later. 'He will wait,' I said to the police when they came to talk to me. 'He will wait. He has to wait until he thinks everyone has forgotten. Then he will start to sell them secretly, probably abroad.' A good Canadian, madame, would never buy these for himself. The police said to me, these are their exact words, 'Let him wait, Professor Le Maître. We will wait, too.'"

"Do you have any idea who did the robbery?" Agatha asked.

"I think so, yes. The police did not confide in me, but I can guess. It was one of three dealers, each of whom had the intelligence and the greed to commit the outrage. There was not sufficient evidence to arrest the man. I believe one of the three has since died. Two are left, and one of them has finally made his move. He will not get away now, thanks to Sandy and Kate."

"Does the name Campeau mean anything to you?" Agatha asked.

"No, Mrs. Bates, it does not."

"Would it be difficult to get any of the pieces out of the country?"

"Not impossible, but very difficult. He cannot use the mail without taking chances, and I am certain he would be watched at the border. Your government would cooperate and search his vehicle thoroughly if we asked. Frankly, I am surprised he has made a mistake at this stage of the game. You understand, Mrs. Bates, that our police will have to talk to you and the girls and anyone else who is concerned."

"I understand, Professor. I hope they will wait a few days. After twelve years, that should not be too long for them to wait."

"We will see. Although Dr. Langhorne did not say so, she intimated that you are a policeman. I should say policewoman."

"I *was* a police officer. I am now a kind of special deputy."

"I thought so. I will ask no more questions. Now, Sandy, now, Kate, let's go into my little museum to make our trade. My collection is not old, but some of it is beautiful, you will see. Most of it is what you might call commercial art. About forty years ago the Inuit carvers organized themselves. They work for money, but so do most artists in the world. The Inuit have to live, too."

Professor Le Maître's museum contained hundreds of sculptures. He explained to the visitors where they came from. He told them he was able to identify the carver for each piece.

"These are imitations," he said, pointing to several pieces. "Not imitations to deceive, mind you, just carvings the artist wanted to look like his ancestors'. I suppose some dealers try to pass them off as real."

"Are these imitations a prohibited export?" Agatha asked.

"No, but a shipment might be examined to see if there are any legitimate old pieces. We must be careful."

Sandy chose a carving of an Inuit mother in a parka with a baby strapped to her back. Le Maître offered Kate a family of owls: Two little ones had their wings outstretched as they squawked at the big owl to be fed.

As they left, Agatha assured the professor that she would be in touch very shortly. "If there is a reward, the Prescotts can use it. And thank you again for your help and the gifts for the girls."

Le Maître's last words were a warning. "I must tell you, Officer Bates, that whoever stole the sculptures committed two crimes the night he broke into the museum. He stole, and he shot a night watchman."

"He killed him?" Agatha asked.

"Not quite. He paralyzed him. He is immobile from the waist down. I recommend caution in your pursuit of this criminal."

24

Arms folded tightly, Lydia Prescott paced Agatha's living room like a tiger in a cage. Duke followed her patiently back and forth, hoping that she would take him for another romp across the playing field, where he would not have to put up with hissing Tom. Every two minutes, Lydia stopped to peer anxiously toward the street.

"Why doesn't Chief Torbert just arrest him and put him in jail? They can make him talk. Or they can give him back to the Canadians."

"For the same reason they couldn't arrest him in Canada, Lydia. We don't have any evidence," Agatha explained patiently. "The only thing we have is the carvings. He thinks he must have them to be safe. They are the bait in our trap."

"And my daughters?" Lydia almost shouted. "What about them? I'm going to call up the Winthrop House and tell them I can't come to work today. I won't leave them. Peggy can look after my tables."

The last thing Agatha needed, if Campeau showed up,

was an angry, anxious Lydia Prescott confronting him. Agatha knew she would not be able to control the situation. She was fairly certain Campeau would make his appearance today or Sunday. He had no reason to wait any longer once he found out the Prescotts were in town. He was bound to be in the vicinity. The afternoon before Duke heard the car outside the Prescott home, a tall, well-dressed man had asked at the general store where the Prescotts lived. Presumably, he called the next day at the mobile home, and perhaps the next two, when Lydia was at work, although no one had seen the Mercedes. Trudeau was now working on finding out where he was staying.

"And that note you say Chief Torbert stuck to our door, Agatha, telling the postman to deliver our mail to your place until our water pump is fixed. You get your mail at the post office, the girls tell me."

"Campeau doesn't know that. Look, Lydia, the man is bound to be restless. All he wants is to find the artifacts and to get back home. He has to be restless. He'll come here today or tomorrow, as soon as he finds the note. I'm sure of it. Now, go to work with Peggy and don't worry. Sandy and Kate are perfectly safe. If we have to, we'll hand over the precious carvings."

Peggy's horn sounded. Duke barked. Tom leaped from the sofa to the mantle. Once again, Lydia asked, "You swear it's all right, Agatha?"

"I swear, Lydia. There is no reason at all for Campeau to harm anyone. We will be all right. Torbert and I are not going to expose your daughters to any danger."

"Torbert will be watching every minute?"

"Yes. Not at my front door, but watching and waiting. We have to make Campeau feel safe, understand? Everything here has to be normal. By now he has found out that you work all day. Torbert will be here the minute we need him. Kate is in charge of that. Now, go on to work. We'll call you the minute we have him. If he doesn't come today, you will be here tomorrow with us, since it's your day off."

Lydia slipped into her coat. She bent down to give Duke a hug. "You be sure to look after Kate and Sandy, Duke," she told him, "and Agatha, too." She smiled bravely and went out to the waiting car.

Agatha watched Peggy's beat-up old car drive away. No other cars were passing the house. She felt alone and apprehensive. It could be a deadly game, she understood. Campeau, or whatever his name was, had killed one man and almost killed another. But all he wanted now, she told herself, were the ancient Inuit artifacts. To get them he would have to explain his partnership with Ralph Prescott, information that she could now only guess at. Even if it wasn't all true, Agatha was confident she could fit together all the pieces.

The police in Henderson were working on banks in Henderson and the towns nearby. Campeau had to have an account somewhere for Prescott to deposit the money he received on sales and deliveries. It had to be in Campeau's name. And it would not be a Canadian bank. By now they would have asked the Canadian police to try to identify the man and his car. But that wouldn't help unless . . .

Unless what? Agatha asked herself. Unless Campeau could be forced to make a mistake. That was what it was coming down to. She and the girls had to draw him into the game and make him feel confident. They would pounce when his guard was down, the way Campeau had pounced on Ralph Prescott at the Twin City Bridge one rainy night.

Sandy and Kate were up. She knocked at their door. "Are you getting dressed?" she called. "Your mother has left for work."

"We're almost ready. We're going to take Duke outside before breakfast."

"Don't go far. Do you want eggs or oatmeal for breakfast?"

Agatha heard Kate groan. "Ugh," she whispered. Louder, she said, "Do you have any cold cereal, please? We're not very hungry, are we, Sandy?"

"I'll see what I have. There's someone out here who wants in, a friend of yours. He has two odd eyes and a bushy tail."

At the table, she asked them one more time if they had it all straight. "If this man comes, he will be very friendly. We will be just as friendly. He has come to see you, not me. Tell him you have the carvings, but not where. Let me handle that. Ask him everything we discussed about your father. He knows more about him than we do. I think he'll tell you the truth.

"Now, Kate, you have the tough part. I figure you can get away with it better than Sandy. The minute Campeau stops being friendly, as he will, the minute he gets tough, you start to cry and run out the door. You know what to say. Don't let him stop you. Run as fast as you can. Sandy says you're the fastest runner in your class."

"I will," Kate said softly.

"That leaves you and me, Sandy. I think we can handle him. We must keep him talking, no matter what. Don't be afraid. We are no danger to Campeau. He will threaten, yes, and we must do what he says."

The phone rang. The three of them jumped. It sounded

151

harsh and threatening. "He's on his way, Agatha," Torbert reported. "Parker just checked him as he went past the gas station. Now he's headed down Old Winthrop Road to the Prescott place."

Agatha looked at her watch. "He should be here by eleven if it works."

"If it doesn't, we'll pick him up and let the Henderson police go to work on him. You and the girls take care, Agatha. This guy is a murderer."

"We'll be careful, Malcolm. Scouts' honor, we'll be very careful."

25

"Get ready," Agatha said. "Sandy, you sit there by the fireplace. Maybe Tom will keep you company. Kate, there's the chair by the door. I'll sit here at the desk. We'll give Campeau the sofa. That's farthest away from the door. Don't forget your milk and toast. You have just gotten up, remember. Where shall we put Duke?"

"I'll take care of him," Kate volunteered. "Give me two pieces of toast. That will keep him close to me."

"Good." Agatha looked at her watch again. "I say he'll be here in three minutes. What do you say, Sandy?"

"Four, I guess."

"And you, Kate?"

"Thirty seconds," Kate said. "I heard a car door shut."

Duke began to growl under his breath. When he heard the tap at the door, he gave a fierce bark.

"Sit, Duke!" Kate ordered. "Sit!"

Duke sat. Agatha went to the door.

"Mrs. Prescott?" a tall, well-dressed man inquired with the slightest of accents.

153

"No, I am Agatha Bates. I am afraid Mrs. Prescott has gone to work. Lydia and the girls are staying here until their water pump is fixed. They need a special part from the factory, Lydia says."

"Do you have any idea when she will return?"

"Not until late tonight. Saturday nights are the busiest nights at the Winthrop House where she works. Not until eleven, I'd say. Is that right, Sandy?"

"That's what it usually is," Sandy replied.

"I see. I did want to talk to her. Perhaps I can talk to the girls. Perhaps they can help me. I knew their father. We were in business together."

"I don't see why not," Agatha said. "They just got out of bed. They are having their breakfast. Why don't you pull your car into the driveway in back of my Toyota. This street is the main road for lumber trucks. There's not much room for them to pass. The town asks us to keep our cars in the driveway."

Agatha stood in the doorway, watching Campeau back his Mercedes into her driveway. A careful man, she thought. He's headed out. It was warm outside for a change. She could smell spring in the air at last. At the side of the house, Henry's tulips were about to bloom. She took Campeau's coat and hung it in the closet.

"Why don't you sit on the sofa," she said. "Would you like some tea? All the coffee I have is the instant kind. Would you like that? This is Sandy Prescott, and that is Kate over there by the door with her dog. His name is Duke."

The stranger bent over to shake hands with Sandy, then with Kate. He bent down to stroke Duke's head. Duke growled. Campeau smiled. "That is as it should be. Never

154

trust strangers. He is a good watchdog. Thank you, Mrs. Bates. No tea, no coffee. I have recently had my breakfast."

Campeau sat easily on the sofa, still smiling. He crossed his legs. "Well, I am very glad to meet Sandy and Kate at last. I am Robert Campeau. Your father may have mentioned me to you. He was my business partner, you might say."

Sandy shook her head. Make the stranger do the talking, Agatha had said.

"He certainly talked about you often enough. He would rather talk about his two girls than business matters."

"Do you have a family, Mr. Campeau?" Agatha asked.

"Regrettably not. Now that I am too old to have one, I believe I made a mistake in staying single." To Kate and Sandy, he said, "I cannot tell you how saddened I was to hear of your father's accident. I did not learn about it until a week later. Even then, I was still in bed with the flu. It was almost pneumonia. I came down to Henderson as soon after that as I could."

Don't let him get away with that, Agatha had told Sandy. "Did Mom call you?" she asked. "She didn't tell us Dad had a partner. And he just told us he was in some kind of business. He never said what. Could you tell us? Kate and I would sort of like to know. We hadn't seen Dad for a while."

Campeau considered how to answer. "No, I did not speak to your mother. I understood from Ralph that affairs were, how shall we say, difficult between the two of them. When I hadn't heard from him for a while, I called the factory. We used the phone on the first floor when we had to. Most of our business we carried on when we met every month. Whoever answered told me he had drowned. I must say again how sorry I am. Your father was a fine man once he, if you will excuse me, once he stopped drinking."

"How did you know Dad?" Kate asked, right on schedule. Agatha was pleased with her actors.

"You might say it was an accident, Kate. Your father walked into my car one night in Henderson. It was a very slight accident. In fact, I was not even aware of it until I was well down the street. I had my car radio turned on. I thought the bump was a noise on the radio at first. I will be honest with you. I kept on driving. I was certain whoever it was wasn't hurt. Since I am a foreigner, I was fearful of becoming involved with your police.

"Later, I felt very bad, let me assure you, and I spared no effort to find out if the person was all right. I located your father in the hospital. He had no money, so I paid his bills, although in no way was I to blame. He had not been badly hurt, just as I suspected."

"So you took him as your business partner," Agatha said, trying not to make her remark sound sarcastic. "That was really very good of you. You must have known that Ralph Prescott had a drinking problem. That is what Lydia and the girls have told me."

"Mrs. Bates, let me tell you something from my own experience. There are alcoholics who stay alcoholics and alcoholics who stop being alcoholics. You can go the good way, if you really want to, or stay the way you are. I was once a drunk, I admit it. It cost me my fiancée. I wasted my inheritance. I lost my friends. One year a long time ago, I was dealing in Eskimo sculptures up north in Hudson Bay. I passed out one night in the street and almost froze to death. An old Inuit craftsman saved me. I will never forget

156

what he said. 'The next time, Monsieur Campeau, I will leave you where you are.' I stopped drinking the next day.

"I told your father the story when I took him from the hospital. 'The next time, Ralph,' I said, 'I won't come back.' I have no reason to believe he took another drink. No, that is not correct. Whenever we met, like two reformed men, we each took a drink of whiskey from a small flask I carry. That was to prove that we were stronger than the alcohol."

"What a fine story," Agatha said. "You must feel that you saved his life."

"In a way, perhaps I did, Mrs. Bates. That is another reason why I grieve so at the terrible accident. Ralph needed something to hang on to, something to give him a purpose. I decided to let him handle my business for me here in New England. I had started to sell my collection of Inuit art. I used to have a shop in the Laurentians. I would always put the very best pieces I purchased from the Eskimos into my personal collection."

"Why did you want to sell them?" Sandy asked. "They're beautiful. I have a seal. Let me show you." Right on schedule. Good for you, Sandy, Agatha said to herself.

Campeau studied the little green seal. "This is an attractive piece. It is not one of mine. I wish it were, Sandy. I could sell it for you if you like."

"No, thank you. I like it too much. Why did you want to sell all of yours?"

"Frankly, I needed money. I recently bought a large apple orchard, and it has been costing me much more than I anticipated. And it consumes all my time. So, I decided I needed a partner in your country."

"Dad liked what he was doing," Kate told Campeau.

"He didn't tell us what he was doing exactly, but he told us about the mill. Why didn't he tell us about the Eskimo carvings? Maybe we could have helped him."

"I think perhaps your father didn't trust himself at first, Kate. He had to be certain he was cured. We found a place in the mill where he could live and work. I advanced him the money. I told him if it worked out, he could open a shop of his own someday. He would know enough by then to buy and sell carvings. Anyway, I took several weeks out of my busy life to get him started. It was apple harvest season for me just then. I was extremely busy. Later, when he was set up, I brought some of my collection down for him to deliver and to sell. After that he drove up to Canada to pick up the works. It saved me time. It was a good arrangement."

"A profitable one for Ralph Prescott, it seems," Agatha noted. "He sent the girls some wonderful presents at Christmas and some money to buy things for their mother."

"It was good for both of us, madame. I had more time for my apple orchard; Ralph had a new start in life. I was more than generous, I believe. Ralph received ten percent for delivery and collecting and twenty-five percent on everything he sold. And, you must remember, I paid for the lease on his place in the mill."

"Lydia was saying she could find no business records among Ralph's things. A lawyer has told her she will need them to clear up the estate."

Campeau paused again before he replied. "Ah," he said, "of course. I should have thought of that. When I drove down to the mill to claim any carvings Ralph had left, I took the records away for my own tax purposes. Please tell Mrs. Prescott I will return them to her promptly."

"Did you find any carvings?" Sandy asked. "We didn't see any on his worktable, only a couple of empty boxes."

"None. He had sold everything I had given him, according to the records. Everything except . . ."

26

"Except what?" Kate asked. "Did Dad lose something?"

"I really don't know. It is very strange," Campeau said, "but I could not find two small ivory carvings I packed for your father to deliver. I had personally sold them. They are copies of two very old Inuit pieces, and they are quite valuable. The design is unique. I acquired them from the man who saved my life that night. They are why I am here. I have been back to the apartment. I have a key. I looked everywhere very carefully. They are not there. The place is empty. I thought to myself, perhaps Mrs. Prescott can help me."

"Do you know anything about two ivory carvings, Sandy?" Agatha asked.

"Do you mean a polar bear with a red mouth and a little knife with animals carved on it?"

"I was right," Campeau said with pleasure. "You do have them. Wonderful!"

"Dad gave them to us, or he was going to give them to us

for our birthdays this summer. We found them wrapped in birthday paper in a box of his clothes."

"Do you have them here?" Campeau asked. "May I see them? Properly speaking, they belong to me. Your father did not understand their true value, I suppose. He put them aside for his girls. He was going to pay me for them from his commissions."

"Gee, I don't know," Sandy said. "They're the last things we had from Dad. We like the modern carvings better, but if Dad wanted us to have these, we'd better keep them. You can take the cost out of the money you owe Dad. Isn't that fair, Agatha?"

Agatha Bates did not reply. She waited.

"But, Sandy, they belong to me. Your father made a mistake. They must be delivered to the person who bought them. I must have them back. I can pay you a reward, I suppose, for finding my property. I can even replace them with two other sculptures from my collection. How about that?"

"No way," Kate shouted. "Sandy doesn't think much of the knife, but I like the bear. You can get another one from the Eskimo."

"We have a problem, Mrs. Bates. Could you intercede with the children to obtain my sculptures? I don't want to go to court about this."

"I don't believe you do, Mr. Campeau. I am sorry, but they *were* left for Sandy and Kate. They showed me the birthday cards taped to the boxes."

Campeau's face took on a stern look. "What are we to do? At least let me see them to be sure they are the missing ones. Are they here?"

"I'm not going to say where they are," Sandy replied. "If I showed them to you, you might steal them from me."

"This is ridiculous," Campeau said in a loud voice. "Mrs. Bates, the children are in your care, it seems. I hold you responsible for their conduct. For the last time, Sandy, bring me the carvings."

"No."

"Then I will do it myself. Where is your room?" Campeau stood up.

"As you say, Mr. Campeau, this is my house. I cannot permit you to search," Agatha said.

"I'm afraid I must, Mrs. Bates." Campeau took a pistol from his pocket. He held it at his side, pointing to the floor.

"I'll get them!" Kate shouted. "They're in our house in Mom's bureau drawer. I'll get them." She ran to the door.

"Stay where you are," Campeau ordered. He headed after Kate. Duke growled deep in his throat. He moved between Campeau and the door. His tail was not wagging. He showed his teeth.

"Sit down, Mr. Campeau," Agatha said pleasantly. "And put that gun away. I don't like guns. I don't allow them in my house. Kate will be back in a little while. Sit down. I'll make you a cup of tea."

"Coffee, please, Mrs. Bates. I am sorry for this scene. I have a permit to carry this gun. I must have it to protect my sculptures when I am traveling."

"I understand, Mr. Campeau. While you are waiting, why don't you read this?" Agatha handed him a copy of her report to Trudeau. "There are a few things I must add, which we learned yesterday from Professor Le Maître. I'll get your coffee."

When Agatha returned, Campeau was sitting quietly on the sofa. The report was on the coffee table, the pistol beside it. Sandy was scratching Duke behind his ears. She looked terrified.

"Here is your coffee. Be careful. It is very hot. The report is essentially correct, is it not, Mr. Campeau?"

Campeau took a small sip of coffee. He put the cup on the table and picked up the pistol. "Yes, essentially. The name is wrong, of course, but that is no longer significant. I don't think we will wait for Kate. Why don't we go to meet her? I will ask you both to escort me out of town. Go to my car, please. I will follow."

"Come on, Sandy. Do as he says." She took Sandy's hand as they went out into the sunshine, Campeau a step behind.

A blue cruiser was parked in front of the Mercedes. Chief Torbert and Deputy Parker MacDonald were leaning against the hood.

"You can't go far in your Mercedes," Torbert called. "Kate has let the air out of your front tire. You can't use our car, either. Someone let the air out of one of our tires, too. Put the gun on the ground real easy and place your hands across the top of that fancy car as far as they will reach."

Campeau did as he was ordered.

"Now, just stay that way, please, until Parker changes our tire. Then we'll pay a visit to Sergeant Trudeau in Henderson. He's waiting to see you. He's found out a few things about you, too, he tells me. Can you hold a gun on him, Deputy Bates? I reckon I'd better help Parker here with the tire. He's not used to police work yet."

163

"Do you have a table for us, Lydia?" Agatha asked when Lydia Prescott greeted them in the reception parlor of the Winthrop House.

"I reserved the best table in the house. It's one of Peggy's. The cook is preparing something special. He won't tell me what. Do I look all right? Peggy lent me one of her dresses."

"You're beautiful, Mom. I brought your new shawl along. I guess it matches. You don't have to work here anymore. Mr. Harper said we are going to be rich."

"Yeah," Kate added. "Real rich. Dad made us rich the way he planned." Her voice shook. "But I wish we had Dad instead of the insurance." Kate buried her face against her mother's shoulder.

Lydia comforted her daughter. Tears came to her eyes. "Why did he do it, Agatha? He didn't have to. Ralph would have given him the carvings."

Agatha turned to Malcolm Torbert, who stood at her side, uncomfortable in a suit and tie. "Why, Malcolm? What did Trudeau say?"

"Ralph wasn't going to give them back, Lydia. He was an honest man. He found out for himself what they were. He knew they had to be stolen, just as Agatha suspected they were. And he knew he was being used to distribute stolen property. He wanted to give Martel—that's Campeau's real name—a chance, like Martel once gave Ralph a chance to set things straight. If Martel didn't listen, Ralph was going to give the carvings to the police. He was too honest, Lydia, and made a mistake. I'm very sorry. We've all made mistakes, I reckon, except Deputy Bates here."

"But, why?" Lydia repeated.

"He didn't want to take a chance on going to jail, Lydia," Torbert answered. "It's not a good place to spend the rest of your life."

Peggy came up to the little group. "Your table's ready, Mrs. Prescott. Come with me, please."